A Bathory Universe Novel

Rise OF THE Monsters

SPECIAL EDITION

Get bitten!

BORN VAMPIRE SERIES BOOK FIVE

ELIZABETH DUNLAP

OTHER BOOKS BY ELIZABETH DUNLAP

Born Vampire Series: Ya Edition (Completed)

Knight of the Hunted (1)

Child of the Outcast (2)

War of the Chosen (3)

Bite of the Fallen (4)

Rise of the Monsters (5)

Time of the Ancients (6)

Born Vampire Series: NSFW Edition (Completed)

Knight of the Hunted (1)

Child of the Outcast (2)

War of the Chosen (3)

Bite of the Fallen (4)

Rise of the Monsters (5)

Time of the Ancients (6)

Born Vampire Short Stories

Tales of the Favored: Arthur's Tale (3.5)

Affairs of the Immortal: The Sinful Affair (4.4)

Affairs of the Immortal: The Knight and Arthur Affair (4.5)

Affairs of the Immortal: The Valentine's Day Affair (6.5)

A Grumpy Fairy Tale Series

The Grumpy Fairy (1)

The Dragon Park (2)

Ecrivain Academy Series

Ecrivain (1)

Neck-Romancer Series

Neck-Romancer (1)

Neck-Rological (2)

Highborn Asylum Series

Freak: A Highborn Asylum Prequel

Stand-Alones

LAP Dogs (coming soon)

PROLOGUE

YEAR: DECEMBER, 2053 - LISBETH

Lisbeth

Running while eight months pregnant was not on my list of fun activities, and yet that's exactly what I was doing. With Arthur in front of me and Knight behind, we moved as a unit down a deserted alley, hoping against hope that the nearby vampire drones wouldn't catch our scent. Arthur stopped at the street opening, waiting, listening. I stood close to his back and tried to ignore how powerful his scent was to me. It was only because of the baby, I kept telling myself.

"You okay?" my mate asked behind me, Knight's warm hands coming around my sides to press on my wide belly. I leaned into him and took a much needed rest for a few precious seconds.

"I'll be better when we're not running so much," I

commented, shutting my eyes and laying my head against his chest.

Arthur shuffled around in front of me and I felt him step closer. "Ssh. They're almost on us." We waited, holding our breath and straining to hear the nearby horde receding. Once they were far enough away, Arthur took my hand as I held Knight's with the other, and we crossed the empty, forgotten street to another alley. Before we were safe in the shadows again, a pain ripped through my belly from deep inside me and I cried out, ruining any chance we had of getting away unseen.

Further down the street I saw them: a pack of several dozen vampire drones, and the creatures roared out a battle cry as they charged towards us. Knight picked me up and dropped me into Arthur's arms, then pushed us towards the alley.

"Go! Get her out of here now!" he commanded, pulling out his pistol and knife, ready to take on the horde to protect us.

To protect me.

"No, no you can't do that!" I shrieked at him, but Arthur was already running in the opposite direction with me in his arms. I pulled myself up to look over his shoulder but we were already too far away to see Knight. "Arthur, no!" I beat at his unwavering shoulders, tears coming down my cheeks. "Put me down, take me back, god damn it!" My protests fell on deaf ears and he continued carrying me away from my mate, so far that I couldn't hear the horde anymore. We went up some stairs and inside an old apartment building. With me still in his arms, Arthur checked every door in the hallway until he found an open one. He carried me inside and set me down in the apartment's entryway.

As he turned back to face me, I slapped him smartly across the face with my full strength, so hard he flew back against the wall and made a dent in it.

"What in the *effing hell* is wrong with you?" I yelled at him, not at all ashamed when his cheek started swelling up from the force of my slap. Arthur righted himself like nothing had happened, lifting his arm to click the apartment door's lock into place and feeling his jaw with his hand. Apparently I'd broken something because it clicked back into place and he tested it a few times by opening and closing his mouth.

"We made a deal," he said once his bones were repaired.

"You *what?*" Glaring into his icy blue eyes, I put my hands on my enlarged hips so he knew how seriously pissed off I was, as if I hadn't made it clear enough already.

"Knight made me promise to protect you, no matter what."

My fists clenched at my sides so hard I smelled my blood. "How many times do I have to tell you to stop making choices for me? You never listen. Never. I don't need you to hold my hand, I don't need you to protect me."

"You asked me to stay by your side and this is what that means."

"Don't you *dare* play that card with me, Arthur. You said you would stay, but you left me." As the words left my lips, I realized how much pain they brought, no matter how much time had passed since it happened.

Arthur continued as if I hadn't spoken. "I will always put your safety over your wishes. I don't care how many times you yell at me, because one day, maybe you'll let me protect you without complaining about it."

Stunned, or maybe just too tired to keep arguing with him, hot tears trickled down my cheeks. "If he dies because of you trying to protect me, I will never forgive you. I forgave you for almost ending his life before. I will not extend that kindness a second time." My anger deflated like a balloon and the tears continued with my hands coming around my belly. The baby kicked at me, almost distracting me from attempting to reach out to Knight with my powers. His image came to my mind, as if I was seeing out of his eyes. He was knee deep in the drones, slashing and shooting when they came at him. I snapped back into my head and wiped my cheeks. "Go get him."

"What, and leave you here, pregnant and defenseless? Absolutely not."

My mouth scrunched up as I contemplated slapping Arthur again. "Why do I even bother pretending you'll do what I say? You never will. You're such an *a-hole*." A rush of hormones brought more tears until I was sobbing against my hands. "I can't lose him again. I can't. I can't..." I broke off into more sobs and Arthur's arms were around me, holding me to his icy warmth in an embrace I hadn't felt for a very long time. That pull to him came again, making me wish he would tilt my chin up and kiss me.

You only want him because of the baby, I told myself over and over. How many years had to pass after Arthur dumped me before I got it through my head that he didn't want me?

"I suppose you made him other promises too," I said quietly against Arthur's chest. One of his large scarred hands stroked at my hair, relaxing me despite my inner turmoil.

"Not the kind you're thinking," Arthur answered.

What did that mean?

I raised my head to ask further when a knock came at the door, startling me out of Arthur's arms. He un-clicked the lock and Knight walked in, covered in blood and ick, but more or less intact. I jumped into his arms, not caring that he was getting blood on me. He was safe, that's all that mattered.

"What happened to your face?" Knight asked, pointing a finger to his cheek, around the same area where Arthur's skin was still mottled.

"She slapped me for taking her away from you," he answered, like it was a normal day for us. To be fair, I'd slapped him before for less.

I grabbed the front of Knight's t-shirt and brought him to me until our noses were pressed together so I could stare right into his deep, brown eyes. "The next time you two make a deal about my safety behind my back, you won't enjoy my reaction either. We clear?"

His Adam's apple bobbed when he gulped at me. "Yes,

ma'am." The stare broke as another sharp pain ran across my stomach and I bent in half from the force of it.

"Owwww..." The word escaped my lips like a timid whine after getting a burr stuck in your foot. The long braid of my hair swung in front of me.

"Oh hell," Knight said quickly, bending to hold my hands. "Is the baby coming?"

I shook my head, letting out a slow breath when the pain passed. I'd been having irregular contractions for the past few days, but nothing serious so far. "Not yet. Soon though."

"This town is crawling with drones," Arthur stated, looking around the apartment. "We'll never make it out alive if they smell that much of your blood." He walked away, checking the apartment for something. Knight led me to a couch in the living room and dusted it off with his hands before helping me sit down.

"Get some rest, we'll keep watch," he assured with a kiss to my forehead. Arthur returned holding a blanket that he draped over me. They stood nearby as I eventually found a comfortable spot despite my round belly and drifted off to sleep.

AFTER WHAT SEEMED like an age of dreamless sleep, I woke up on the couch with Knight sleeping in an easy chair nearby. Arthur stood by one of the windows, looking out at the street. He noticed me sitting up and stretching, and he came to sit at the end of the couch by my feet. With me distracted by a yawn, he took my foot in his hands and removed my shoe to press his fingers into my swollen skin.

"Do..." he started, and stopped, hesitating, which was not like him at all. "Do you recall the last time I rubbed your pregnant feet?" His eyes stayed downwards, focused on his task, which was nice because I'd started turning pink with that particular memory coming to the forefront of my mind. So many years ago, Arthur had rubbed my feet when I was pregnant with Kitty, and then he kissed me so deeply, so passionately, it wasn't hard to realize I'd fallen in love with him. Unsure of what his intentions were with this conversation, I stayed silent, except for the soft sighs escaping my lips whenever he pressed just right. "When I left to search for Alistair, I told Knight that if you had the second child in your dream while I was gone that he needed to massage your feet every night."

I giggled mid-sigh. "That's why he was so insistent about doing that when I was expecting Jason. He must've liked the suggestion."

"Actually he told me he was planning on it anyway. Said he needed to take care of you for both of us." Arthur moved to my other foot, removing my shoe, and drawing a hiss from me when he pressed into my arch. "I'm..." He hesitated again and my stomach flipped over with either dread or anticipation. I couldn't tell which. Both. "I'm sorry I left you. You were right earlier, you asked me to stay by your side and I left." Just barely, his eyes turned towards me, but he refused to meet my gaze.

"You had to—"

"I didn't have to," he interrupted. "I was trying..." He finally met my eyes with his icy, blue irises. "I was trying to forget you." My stomach flipped again, and dread was the emotion that stayed. Of course he wanted to forget me. He didn't want me like that anymore. His insistence on me being with Knight was proof of that. Embarrassed, I tried to take my foot back but he refused to let it go. "It didn't work, Lisbeth." That stopped me, freezing my body on the couch. My eyes moved to where Knight lay, still asleep. Even though the thought of him hearing this had my heart skipping a beat, I wished he was awake because I felt as fragile as a bird egg. "It's impossible to forget you. You're etched into every part of me."

"Stop," I said, getting up and holding my round belly to steady myself. "You can't say these things to me." The words felt like poison leaving my lips. I wasn't even sure if I meant them. It was a programmed response, a product of my upbringing in a society that no longer existed. A curtain of tears smudged the image of Arthur on the couch, staring up at me. "You pushed me away. You said you didn't want me."

"I lied."

"*Damn it*," I swore, bringing a hand up to my trembling lips as two simple words changed everything inside me. I wiped my eyes and looked away to bring myself together. He stood up so I held out a hand between us. "Stay. You stay there," I ordered firmly. If he touched me, I would be lost, and I didn't want that. Not right now when everything was uncertain inside my head. "You don't get to reject me and then say it was a lie after *thirty-five years*." My hand moved to point at Knight's sleeping form. The mental connection between us was silent, making me confident he wasn't faking and was actually asleep. "He would never do that to me. You think you know what's best for me, but you never stop to think that you're wrong. You don't listen to me about anything. About what I want. About what I need from you. Regardless of whether or not Knight approves of you being my mate, I can't be with you if you act like that. And even if you changed..." My eyes fell to the apartment carpet, stained with dirt from the family that lived here before the world ended. "Part of me thinks you're too late."

"And the other part?"

I looked back up and met his eyes again, the turmoil inside me only rising at the sight of his scarred face. "Prove to me you can change and we'll see." My belly came alive with another rip of pain and I braced myself against the chair Knight was sleeping in, startling him awake.

"What happened? Is it the cat again?" The pain increased and I screamed as a flush of water flowed down my legs. Knight swore, hopping out of the chair. Despite our heated conversation, Arthur was next to me in an instant, holding me steady with his arms. Even after me telling him I might not want him anymore, I clung to him like a lifeline, and the warmth in my chest at being so close to him had me desperate to never let him out of my arms.

"Gather our stuff," Arthur told him, and Knight left to get our bags as a contraction started in my lower belly. My husband returned with our meager belongings in his hands. "We should try to leave town as fast as we can. If you're okay with it?" He gave me a meaningful look and Knight raised an eyebrow at him in confusion.

"The hell happened to you?"

"Great effort, terrible timing," I admonished, gripping Arthur's arm during some intense baby kicks. "I'll tell you if you're being a butt face, just get us out of here." Nodding, he took the bags from Knight who picked me up, soggy clothes and all, and I wrapped my arms around his neck to keep myself upright. Arthur unlocked the apartment door and checked the hallway before signaling we follow him. Knight followed behind him, holding me close, until we reached the stairwell. We went down several flights of stairs and out to the apartment lobby where Arthur checked the street outside from the lobby door window.

"You get the urge to scream, bite down on Knight, but try not to draw any blood," Arthur said, his eyes trained on any movement outside. "Knight, don't stop running for anything. There's a gas station outside town that we passed on our way in that should be far enough away from the drones. If we get separated, take her straight there. I'll meet you as soon as I can."

What if he didn't come back?

The thought hung between us as he met my eyes, and I saw a wave of emotions pass over those two globes of ice.

"I didn't mean what I said," I told him feebly, feeling my tears threatening to come back.

"You did." He blinked a few times and turned back to the front door. "Get ready, Knight. There's a pack down the street. If we're quiet enough, we might be able to slip past them. And... go." He ripped the door open and held it for us to pass through. Knight creeped down the apartment building steps, only pausing for a second once we reached the sidewalk as we saw the horde of drones walking aimlessly around a crosswalk a few blocks over.

Another contraction started and I squeaked slightly, trying to hold it in before planting my mouth on Knight's shoulder and biting down hard. Even with my fangs retracted, I still made a dent in his shirt, but managed to not break his skin. Arthur led us in a hurried rush down the street, away from the drones. I hoped against hope the baby wouldn't pop out right there and ruin our escape.

Stay inside, baby. Just a little longer, I sent to the infant inside me. Similar to when I'd been carrying Kitty, she cooed at the sensation of being connected to me. I felt a reaction back from her that assured me she wasn't coming just yet. There was enough time to get to safety. We stopped at the end of the street and Arthur listened, sniffed, looked around.

"There's a group of them really close to us. We have to be careful." He motioned for us to cross the street at a different point so we'd be as far away as possible. All hopes were squashed, because the scent of fresh blood filled the air like a beacon. My blood. Arthur took out his rifle, standing between me and the horde that was quickly waking up from my scent. "Get her out of here."

Knight took off in the other direction and I rested my chin on his shoulder to keep my eyes on Arthur as long as possible. We rounded the corner of a building just before the mob overtook him. Labor distracted me too much for me to push my senses out, making me feel blind and deaf to the outside world, unable to assure me Arthur would be okay. I clutched Knight's neck tightly, trying to keep myself together during another contraction.

My mate was silent until we made it to the gas station outside of town. He kicked the boarded up door in, setting me down once we were inside and he righted the boards just in case something followed us. I leaned against the large countertop with the cash registers, wiping at the sweat on my forehead. Knight came up behind me and started rubbing my lower back, right where it was hurting. The touch of his hands was a balm on my pain, both physical and emotional.

"He'll be okay," Knight soothed, kissing my exposed neck.

"I'm getting very tired of you two risking your life for me," I groaned as I lowered my head between my spread hands.

"Can't stop, won't stop." Something banged against the gas station door like a bird flying into a window. Knight approached, sniffing the air. "What's the password?"

"For god's sake, let me in!" Knight opened the wooden boards and Arthur entered the gas station looking no worse for wear, like we'd left him at a shoe store instead of facing a drone mob. He gave me a significant look before glancing down at my belly. "Let's find the freezer. It'll be safest in there."

They both herded me to a metal freezer near the bathroom. With electricity long gone, it was warm inside, and our enhanced sight allowed us to see even when the door was closed and locked. Knight laid out my sleeping bag and helped me sit on it. I automatically reached for Arthur's hand when Knight turned to rummage through his duffel.

"Been a while since we were here, right?" I joked to the vampire beside me, trying to smile through the pain. "Good thing you've both helped me during labor before. Makes me feel better about not having a doctor around."

Even as I squeezed his hand during another contraction, Arthur still managed to look stoic. "I feel obligated to point out that I'm an actual doctor, but thanks for the confidence."

Knight produced a cloth that he soaked with some of our precious water, and he mopped at my sweaty forehead with it. "General Doctor Lancaster," he snarked under his breath. "If you tell me you're also a Duke, I'm going to lose my shit."

That silenced the vampire, lips pressed together, his hand still clutched in mine. "Okay. Then I won't say that."

"*Oh my god.*"

"Can you two stop making out and focus?" My protest ended with another painful contraction that I screamed out, squeezing Arthur's hand so hard I heard his bones creak. He didn't cry out, he simply leaned in and kissed my sweaty temple like I would shatter if he pressed too hard. It made my heart squeeze almost as painfully as the contractions that now seemed as if no time was passing from one to the next. Knight kissed the other side of my head, making me a Lisbeth sandwich. Arthur stood up, and together both men helped me stand. Knight's arms came up from behind me to hold me upright while Arthur removed my underthings.

Groaning, then laughing, I leaned into Knight's warm body and smiled down at Arthur's blonde head. "Not exactly how you pictured getting my pants off, I bet."

"Teasing Arthur, you must be delirious," Knight said beside my ear.

"I'm allowed a few quips with the excuse that I was in serious pain." And I was. I was in so much pain I knew my third baby was about to emerge. Through the haze of agony, I focused on Arthur seated between my knees. "What was her name?"

He glanced up at me and didn't even have to ask who I meant. The woman he was mated to before I knew him. "Adriann." I hadn't even thought up baby names. Vampires tended to choose after the baby was born. "Don't name it after her. I failed her. I won't fail this baby." He took my offered hand just as my pain crested.

Sound disappeared around me. Everything focused on the baby coming, with Knight urging me on and Arthur ready to catch her. My body was only pain, only thirst, only feeling, until my thirst was the only thing I remembered. Both men were ready for it, as it had happened before. The soft mewling cries of an infant were lost to me because I needed blood like I needed air, and I turned lightning fast in Knight's arms, slamming him against the freezer wall and sinking my fangs into his hot neck, pulling enough blood to bring my clarity back.

"Don't stop until you're healed," Arthur barked behind me amidst more of the tiny wails. I took a long drink of Knight's blood with one hand pressed to his pulse to assure me I wasn't draining him. The pain in my extremities slowly dissipated like it never happened and I slumped against Knight's chest after withdrawing my fangs. His arms came around me and we sank to the metal floor, both exhausted and drained in more ways than one.

Arthur approached holding a bundle wrapped in some blankets we'd kept with us for this moment: the moment when I met the third child from my vision. He handed her to me carefully and sat in front of us, watching her like a hawk. She had soft blonde hair like her father, and a pout to match his stoic face. When she opened her eyes, they were two bright, blue circles, like soft, blue pansies.

"She's exactly like my vision," I said in a hushed whisper, and leaned in to kiss her warm forehead. Arthur met my gaze when I looked up at him, an almost smile on his icy face. I leaned in, kissed his scarred cheek, and hugged him with my free arm. "Thank you for giving her to me." The warmth for him was still there, deep inside my breast, but I wasn't ready to confront what he'd said to me. I had more important things to deal with, like naming my new baby girl. Back against Knight's warm embrace, I stared down at our daughter's chubby, pink face. "Alexander gave his life to protect us. If it wasn't for his generosity all those years ago, neither of you would be here right now."

Knight gently pressed his lips to my temple again and drew my face to his with a finger on my chin, kissing me with more passion than he usually showed me in front of Arthur. He pressed our noses together and stroked at my cheek with his hand, sending tingles all over my tired body. "Regardless of that stupid bracelet, I wouldn't have hurt you. I have no doubt you would've won me over eventually."

"I would've brought you in either way, so there's that," Arthur cheeked, making Knight toe him with his shoe as punishment.

Smiling at their antics, I looked back down at the baby in my arms, watching her yawn widely. "I'd like to name her Alexandria. Dreya for short." I glanced up for confirmation and both men nodded in approval. "It's settled then. And soon, her brother and sister will be back with us. We'll be together again." My heart painfully twisted again from being separated from my other children, not to mention the rest of our family. I had to believe that one day we'd find them and they would never leave us again.

"Rest," Arthur ordered softly. "We'll leave the family hunt to another day." He stood and busied himself with gathering our things. If we stayed too long after spilling this much blood, the drones would swarm like a hive of bees. There was enough time to rest and feed Dreya before we had to go.

I'd allow myself enough time for Dreya to grow old enough not to cry out and alert the drones, but then we had to continue searching for Kitty and Jason, or I was going to lose my mind with worry.

Soon. I'd be with all my babies soon.

1

IN A KINDLY MOOD

YEAR: 2073 - KITTY

A dust storm greeted me on the edge of the bleeder city. I'd just rolled into town after weeks of searching for the place. With dust swirling in the air like someone had turned on a dry ice machine, my bandana and goggles protected my face from the worst of it, but it made visibility of the town so low I could barely see two steps in front of me. A quick sweep with my enhanced senses showed me the path, and I stepped into the clouds with confidence. Pieces of glass chinked against my boots from various broken windows along the street. The old road pavement was cracked, and weeds were pushing through the asphalt. Twenty years of neglect will do that to concrete. The further I walked through the town, the more damage I could see, even through the puffs of dirt.

A ghost town. That's what they would've called it in the

past. Except this town was merely *almost* abandoned. Not quite there yet. There were still a few bleeders to go around, and sharks a plenty up in the hills.

Eventually, the broken road led to my destination: the only building that smelled like warm bodies. The double door entrance was locked, with good reason considering I was one of the monsters the bleeders were trying to keep out. I lifted my slightly dirty hand and rapped on the wood a few times, hearing the sound echo. Movement inside suggested the bleeders were awake, and they knew sharks didn't waste time knocking. One stepped up to the door. I smelled steel and gunpowder, and the sweet stink of fear.

"State your business!" a man shouted. "Drinker, mutt, or human?"

My mouth curled at his slurs, but I was in a kindly mood today. "Drinker." I risked being turned away revealing my true nature like that, even at a backwater place like this.

The sound of wooden slats being moved grated my ears, and the door creaked open before the bleeder stuck out the barrel of his rifle. "No guns."

I scoffed. "You take Artemis from me and we'll have a problem, son." Behind him, someone ordered to let me in, and the door opened enough for me to do so before the bleeder closed it and replaced the wooden barricades.

The building had once been a saloon, apparently, and a man stood behind the mahogany bar wiping a glass with a towel like this was a normal day. I dusted my vest and pants, emitting puffs of dirt, and slipped my bandana off my chin and my goggles onto the crown of my head. My face had to be a frightful state with all the dust in the air. I'd worry about it later.

"What can I do you for, drinker?" the bartender inquired, watching me out of the corner of his eye. "Don't see many of your kind around these parts. Not decent ones, anyhow." He set his cup down and started wiping another. Was he busying himself out of fear, or did he really need to be cleaning all that glass just now? "What's your name?"

I stepped up to him, my boots clunking on the floor with every move, and I sat at one of the green bar stools. "Don't see how that's your business, bleeder."

"Now, now," he cautioned, and I heard the man behind me gripping his rifle again. "No need for name calling here."

Grabbing one of the newly cleaned glasses, I poured myself a shot of whatever he had on the counter. "You started it, friend. Drinker. Mutt. How am I supposed to take that kind of talk?" I raised an eyebrow at him and downed the shot like it was water. For me it practically was.

"Fair enough." He nodded and his friend put the rifle down. "My apologies. Place like ours, we like to keep a list of names in case anyone comes looking. Nice way to make money."

Inhaling deeply, I smelled what I'd come for. Night Shadow. "Not the only way, I heard." He leveled me with a stare but said nothing. "I can smell your stash. I'm willing to do business."

He gave me a once over. "You don't seem like the type. Most of them aren't so... put together."

"Judge someone else, you're wasting your time. I'll trade you a pint of blood for ten ounces, and some information."

Laughing, he poured himself a shot and downed it. "Your blood would have to be worth gold to fetch a price like that, darlin'."

"I can assure you, it is. In fact, my blood is worth every bit of product you have."

He laughed more and poured us both shots before he leaned in to me, so close I could smell he'd eaten honeyed carrots for lunch. Business must be booming if he could afford honey. Or carrots. "Let me see your eyes." Unflinching under my blue and purple stare, what he found there brought a smile to his face. "They told me about you. I didn't believe it. The golden goose of vampires. Your blood makes the best product we've ever seen." He leaned back and tapped his finger against his glass. "Five ounces for a pint."

"Eight. And the information." He raised his glass, and we toasted in agreement. I couldn't help but feel a bit of disgust in the act, doing business with a man like him. I could smell what kind of man he was, like he was wearing it as a sign around his neck. Desperate times and all.

"What information would that be?" he inquired.

"My name is Kitty Bathory, and I'm looking for my mother."

TWENTY YEARS. Twenty years since I'd seen my mother's face, since she bid me farewell at the airport and I'd given her husband our first fist bump. Sweet, loving Knight. He'd raised me and all I ever showed him was contempt. I'd been such a child. If I never saw either of them again, I'd have to live with the knowledge that I'd never told Knight I loved him.

Then there was my real father, the Incubus Balthazar. I also hadn't seen him in twenty years, no surprise there. He had always been flighty, even if his love for me kept him coming back. He hated being tied to one spot, to see the same walls for any amount of days in a row. I'd asked him many times why that was, but he never gave me a straight answer. Mother said that he loved her grandmother, the Countess of Bathory. With that, I'd concluded that something about her death had altered him. So, as much as I wanted to, I couldn't resent him for leaving me. Well, I could, but it made me feel very guilty.

As if I didn't have enough people to miss, the last person in my family had also been gone for twenty years: Jason, my half-brother. He'd been just a kid when I left, with his long, poufy hair that threatened daily on turning into an afro, and not the fashionable kind. Before communication was cut off, I'd been told he was going off with Balthazar to be safe, and honestly the thought of my dad raising anyone on his own had my stomach in knots. If Balthazar flaked, had anyone been there to care for Jason? Had he grown up alone? Out of all four of the people that consumed my thoughts, I felt the most guilt over Jason. Having him grow up in this new world, potentially alone, I could barely stomach the thought without doubling over in agony.

The one and only thought that comforted me was Arthur. Arthur would keep them all safe. I would've too, if I could only find them. I wasn't the insecure teenager I used to be. If anyone messed with me, they met the wrong end of Artemis, and she could blow a hole through anything.

All of that ran through my head as I stared at the bleeder behind the bar and took another shot after asking about my mother.

"Looking for a drinker, is it?" he asked with a smug grin.

"Mutt, actually."

He reached under the bar, I stilled and laid one hand on Artemis just in case he pulled something out that shot bullets, but he produced a very dirty notebook that could've used some serious wet wipes. He ran a hand over it, but it just made the dirt smears worse. Another shot, just to wash the taste of dirt from my tongue. It didn't work. The bartender opened the notebook and started flipping through pages that had plastic protectors on them, probably to keep the dust out. It wasn't called the 'Dust Bowl' for nothing. "Mutts. Here we are. Name?"

"Knight. Like in shining armor." I wasn't sure which name my mother would be going by, since she tended to flip back and forth between 'Lisbeth,' 'Erzsébet,' and 'Elisabeth' depending on who she was talking to. No matter what name she had, she would never be without Knight. Unless he was dead.

The bleeder licked a finger —gross— and flipped more pages. "Nope, no mutts with that name. Anyone else?"

"Arthur. Drinker." Assuming Arthur was still with her. She'd lose him before Knight, but if Knight was gone, Arthur would never leave her side. Not even to take a piss.

More flips, more gross finger licks. Was he trying to attract me with his tongue? It wasn't working. "Arthur. Here's one. He passed this way... hmm." He bent close to the paper and then lifted it up for the other bleeder to look at. "Slim, that a six or an eight?"

Slim. Gods, how cliché could this crowd be?

Slim bent over the bar and squinted at the slightly smudged numbers. "That's a five. Learn to read, idjit." Slim got a smack on the head with the notebook before it was stowed back under the counter.

"Your friend came through here fifteen years ago." I raised my eyebrows at him. They'd kept records for that long? "Sorry I couldn't be more helpful, girlie."

"Call me that again and I'll be leaving here with your entire stash as you bleed out on the floor."

"No need to be touchy, *girlie.*"

Well. I *did* warn him.

A few bullets later, I had his stash, his money, and I grabbed a full bottle of tequila on my way out as I stepped over their worthless corpses.

Guess this place was a ghost town after all.

2

A FAMILIAR FACE

KITTY

*W*ith the dust outside to greet me, I stepped back over the broken glass and up to my motorcycle. Pulling my goggles back down and my bandana up, I stashed my haul into my backpack. Though I didn't do it often, I'd left it on the cycle because I knew there wasn't anyone around to mess with it. Plus, if things had gone south in the saloon —well, *more* south to be precise— I didn't want to risk my supplies. I lifted one boot and straddled my ride before slinging the backpack over my shoulders and clipping it in front to stay put.

A push on the pedal to start the roaring engine, and I left the town and the fresh corpses in the dust where they belonged.

As I picked up speed, the wind whisked at the parts of my face that were still uncovered. My hair in its long braid was tempted to come undone despite it being tied fast like Thalia taught me. The mere memory of her was enough to sober me, but I stayed focused on the road and ignored the slight fog on my goggles.

Focus, Kitty. The information from the bleeders wasn't what I'd hoped. My plans were basically ruined, and I was back to square one. I'd been following a lead to my parents for three years straight only for it to end like this. From one back water hell hole to the next, buying drugs and information in exchange for my blood. I never gave more than that, and if anyone expected more, they met Artemis. The world didn't need more villains in it, and I happily played the anti-hero. Robbing from the assholes and giving to myself. Robin Hood with no morals. Kitty Hood.

Before the apocalypse, I hadn't needed to kill anyone. Alistair had taken that from me. From everyone. I was already a monster, and I slipped into the role with ease. First with the misfits I'd left home with, and then on my own.

When was the last time I'd had an actual conversation with someone worth talking to? My perfect memory told me the real number, but I pretended not to know because it had been *so effing long.*

Sometimes I had conversations in my head. With family. With friends. With imaginary people. I knew I was insane, just a little. But really, who wasn't these days? Insanity ran in the Bathory line, so I had to carry on that legacy somehow.

I burned rubber for hours until the sun began to set. My cycle ran on solar power, but it also wasn't safe to be around after dark. At night, the sharks were heightened. Darkness was their hunting ground. I pushed my senses out and found a spot that was far away from any shark clusters. As long as I didn't spill any blood and left within a few hours, they would leave me alone. Hopefully.

Deep in a dense forest, I propped my cycle up against a tree and reached inside the engine for a very small component that I added to the chain around my neck. The vehicle wouldn't work without it, and if anyone saw the part around my neck, they would think it was just a simple charm. It had saved my cycle from being stolen many times over the years. Bleeders tended to not steal something that didn't work. Folks had to be on the move these days so they couldn't lug around a scrap of metal hoping it would come in handy, and anyone who was smart enough to know what parts to steal never lived long enough to grab their wrenches.

With my cycle safe, I pulled out my little pop up tent from my backpack and it sprang up as soon as I'd taken it out of its bag. After one quick check with my senses just to be sure I was alone, I laid out my blanket on the vinyl fabric floor before zipping up the tent behind me. After cleaning my face off and removing my vest, I grabbed the bleeder's stash before closing my backpack and placing it at the head of my blanket for a pillow. The front pocket held one of my few luxuries, a second blanket. Since I never got cold, its sole purpose was to keep the backpack from being too lumpy under my head. Without that scrap of fleece, my bag was lumpy in all the wrong places and I never got a lick of sleep.

Plushness under my head, I leaned up on one elbow and opened the large Ziplock baggie of Night Shadow and pulled out two red-purple colored pills. Seeing them in my fingers was unsettling enough to make me feel sick to my stomach, but I did this for a reason. Before I could change my mind, I popped the first pill in my mouth and dry swallowed it with a sigh.

The effect took a minute as I was not the intended species they were made for. It hit like a slam against the wall and the tent was spinning and shiny and I wasn't sad anymore. Not sad about Jason, or my mom, or both of my dads, or Thalia. Everything was as happy and peaceful as it had been before, when I was a moody little girl in her stupid black hoodie.

As the spinning slowed and the shiny grew, a tear ran down my cheek despite the false endorphins I was feeling, and they felt amazing, I will say. Being on Night Shadow was like my nights with Thalia. Bright and explosive with pleasure.

My sweet Thalia.

Coughing, I sat up and the high disappeared. Stupid genetics. I could never enjoy the high for more than... I checked my watch. An hour had passed. It felt like thirty seconds.

In the bitter aftertaste, I saw a face in my mind: the vampire whose blood had made that particular Night Shadow pill. I never saw the Lycan's face even though both blood types were needed to make the drug.

The vampire's face was unknown to me, like all the rest

had been for all the years I'd been a drugged-out loser in a stupid attempt to find my mother.

Damn it.

Angrily, I tossed the baggie of pills somewhere by my feet and popped the second one in my mouth, biting into it with one of my fangs. The sweet liquid was like heavenly acid and I swallowed it down, waiting for the high to wash away my feelings.

Shiny, shiny tent. Make a mirage of someone. Anyone. You can do it, tent.

"Kitty?" a voice called.

Oh great. Now you do what I want when I'm too tweaked out to open my eyes. Stupid tent. The high was going away and the face that came to me made me shoot up from my bed.

Mother.

3

MEMORIES OF THEN

KITTY

As soon as the sun came up, I was off on my cycle going back to the ghost town to check the bleeder's records. If he had a record of every vamp, Lycan, or bleeder's presence over the past umpteenth years, he was sure to have a record of where he got his product or who had donated blood.

After two pills of Night Shadow, I was feeling a bit hung over, but only just. I needed blood. Without a steady supply of regular food or water, blood was my only daily requirement. I'd have drunk the bleeders dry, except as a Vipyre, the only Incubus and Vampire hybrid in existence, I drank vampire blood. Sharks were becoming my only food supply now, but they didn't really sate my hunger the way vampires did. I was always thirsty.

Soon I was back where my journey ended. I'd been stupid enough to leave the bodies inside the saloon, having not intended to return, so a cluster of sharks had arrived to pick at the corpses.

Great.

The dust storm was long passed, and the cracked, weed ridden street stood between me and the sharks. They'd already cleaned the bodies out, but they were still standing in the doorway and around the porch like mannequins. The monsters were pretty stupid. Unlike real sharks, they didn't just leave after the kill. They stuck around because there was only air between their ears. Air and fangs. Fangs that were in my way, and I didn't take to anything that stood in my way.

I counted about twenty of them, a small group if I ever saw one. I'd been amongst hundreds before. That solemn memory slowed my hand on Artemis, and I pointed my chin up to wipe the sadness away. Tucking my bottom lip under my top teeth, I let out a shrill whistle, the one I'd learned from an old friend.

The sharks enraged at the sound mixed with the smell of fresh blood. They charged at me, but I was ready for them. As the first came close, I put a hand up to flip over its back and fired a shot off with Artemis in its stomach. That would slow it down for now. The second came at me and tried to wrestle me into its grip. I stuck my barrel up its chin and fired, then turned a sharp left to stop the blood and bits from getting on me. His body fell and the third shark used it as a step up to jump on me, so I tore into the shark's neck with my fangs and drank deep of his blood to sate my hunger. After a few long pulls, I ripped out a piece of his neck with my teeth and spat it to the ground before shoving him away.

They all rushed me like a swarm of bees and I laid them to waste, by either Artemis or my fangs. I'd need to burn the bodies to make sure more sharks wouldn't come, just in case I had to come back. Later, though. I had other things to do first.

With Artemis cocked in my hand, I filled her with more bullets from my belt as I approached the saloon. The doors were wide open but I didn't spot any shark stragglers from the horde. The two bleeder bodies I'd left looked like they'd been attacked by vultures. Only the skeletons and their clothes were left.

Gross. Sharks were such nasty creatures.

I stepped around the bones and hopped up onto the counter, poured myself a shot of whatever was out, and landed with a click of my boots on the other side of the bar. Downing another shot, I found the notebook the bartender had shown me, as well as a few other equally dirty ones. I should've brought them with me in the first place. I supposed the utter disappointment had clouded my brain. Normally I was on point with my actions. I needed to get back to that level of smart, and fast. At least I didn't need to take Night Shadow anymore, but I'd still keep the stash for trading fodder. It would get me miles more in trades than my blood could, seeing as how not everyone knew how to make the drug, but most everyone wanted it.

With the notebooks in my backpack, and a few odds and

ends I found in the saloon, I piled all the sharks into a stinking pyre and set it up in flames before leaving the way I'd come.

A FEW HOURS OF ROAD, several shots of the strongest liquor I could find, and a new camp set up in a dilapidated high riser, I finally had the time to look at the bleeder's records. I propped myself up against a wall that was once where hundreds of workers came to their worthless jobs every day before the sharks came and ruined everything. The air no longer held the metallic scent of blood, but I was certain carnage had happened on the very floor I sat.

Another shot of the liquor I'd brought with me, and I opened the notebook to look for clues. The bleeder's last shipment of Night Shadow had been three weeks before, and the supplier was... anonymous. What the hell was an anonymous supplier? Were we in the days of law enforcement when drugs were outlawed? Hardly. I sighed and slammed the book down to run my fingers through my long black curls.

My eyes immediately went to my backpack where the baggie of Night Shadow sat. I didn't need it. I *didn't*. Except... I enjoyed being taken away from my life, from this hell I spent all of my waking hours in. The hell where my family is probably lost forever, where Thalia is dead, and I'm alone. Just alone. *Always alone.* Choking back a sob, I grab my bag and put two Night Shadows in my mouth, crushing them with my teeth and feeling the drug take hold like the temptuous bite of a snake.

I'm back home. Jason is sitting at the kitchen table next to me playing something on his holographic game console. Balthazar is kissing Toni on the cheek and he gives me a blue-eyed wink when I catch his eye. *Dad.* I want to reach out to him and hold him close but he's not really here. Before the spell can be broken, I look to my left and see Mom leaning in to kiss Knight on the lips as she sets down a plate of fried chicken for dinner. She sees me staring and chuckles before planting a comforting kiss on my head.

"What's the matter, Kitty?"

I almost knock my chair over in my haste to stand and throw myself into her arms. She smells so good, like flowers and bread. "I don't know. I just missed you." Letting her go, I wipe my cheeks and surrender as the fantasy takes over.

"Dweeb," Jason murmurs, kicking me slightly with his foot when I sit back down. He's such an adorable jerk. I steal a piece of chicken from his plate and sink my fangs into it triumphantly before sticking my tongue out and showing him my partly chewed food. Without missing a beat, he steals from my plate too and repeats my see-food display with a giggle.

"They're *so* mine," Knight says happily from across the table. Closing my mouth, I look back at him and relish the sight of his face.

"I love you, dad," I say to him, and I feel my lips say the

words outside of my fantasy where the real world lies. Knight flaps his hand over Mom's arm excitedly.

"*She called me dad!*" he squeaks. "Imma cry!" I hand him some of my chicken, just because, even though he has a full plate. "Up top, kiddo!" He holds out his hand and as I reach up to slap it, the fantasy snaps closed and I'm back in the real world, standing in one of the open windows with my hand out ready to high five the empty air.

No, come back. Come back to me. A tear rolled down my cheek and I closed my hand before letting it fall to my side. I could still smell Mom's scent like she was standing beside me, could still feel the softness of Jason's hair, still see everyone's face with aching clarity.

My heart was aching, my body was tired, I wasn't sure how much longer I could stand this.

Meow.

Artemis flashed out and I turned to see a cluster of cats in the room with me. They were unimpressed by my gun. Several had made a bed on my stuff and I spotted a crowd inside my tent. First a horde of sharks, and now a horde of fluffy kitties.

I stuffed Artemis back into her holster. "Hi, kitties. I'm Kitty." The room smelled like warm cat. One of them came up and rubbed against my legs so I crouched to scratch under its chin, but it ran from me before I could touch it. "Guess you guys have never seen a person before. Don't let me fool you. Not all the creatures out there are as nice as me."

They didn't seem to care. I went to my bed after moving the cats out of the way and fell asleep to the sound of purrs.

4

DON'T CALL ME GIRLIE

KITTY

The next morning, I woke to a pair of yellow eyes in my face. A black cat sat staring at me like he had nothing better to do. His long black tail swished back and forth, no doubt his brain's way of deciding whether to pounce on me or not. The horde of felines was probably descended from house cats and had made this tower their home. They had birds, water, rats. I bet they'd never been outside of the structure.

"Morning," I said out loud to the observing cat, saluting it with my fingers to my forehead. Slowly, I reached a hand out to pet him and he let me for a few moments. So soft and warm. The first real body I'd touched in years. After a few strokes on his head, he'd had enough, and he scurried away from sight. "I just wanted to pet you, geez!" I turned and came face to face with a white cat lounging on my hip.

Forget shark invasion, this was a cat invasion!

Amid protests, I shoved the cats away and stood up to stretch. Okay. I needed a plan. Plans were all I had, and I wasn't about to give up and become a crazy cat lady. The cats hadn't managed to gobble up my food yet, so I settled down on the floor with the last bits of my dried fruit in one hand and the ledger in the other. Since the latest shipment was a bust, I just had to make my way backwards. There were about ten other suppliers with only one mentioned several times. The bleeder might've been greasy looking, but he kept detailed records. He even had a location for all the suppliers on the back page. It made sense since phones no longer worked.

Ah, phones. How I missed texting.

Mom, where r u?

Jason, ur not 2 cool 4 school.

Knight, I borrowed your razor to shave my legs.

Dad, you suck incorporeal butt.

Arthur, stop mooning over my mom and kiss her already.

I packed up my stuff, now all covered in cat hair, and started down the hallway. Several cats followed me. Maybe they thought I was their leader. A vampire was totally part cat part human. We both had fangs, at least. Once I hit the stairs, the cats stayed behind to continue their lives in the tower without me. Maybe I'd come back and steal a kitten or two. Who knew how much they'd get me in the right city? Everyone loved cats. A puppy though, that would've been worth its weight in gold. Most dogs had gone feral or rabid after the sharks came, and people were very hard up for guard dogs. I figured a barn cat would hold the same value if I found a farm.

Just as I'd reached the bottom floor, I turned to reconsider going back up and finding where they'd stashed the kittens. Sitting on the last step was the black cat with yellow eyes, still staring at me.

"Puss," I said in salute again. Maybe he knew I was considering taking their babies. They sent him to spy on me. Fluffy jerks. "I won't take the babies. I'm leaving. Bye." I rolled my eyes and wondered at my sanity for addressing a cat like it could understand me. My boots crunched on the lobby floor and I left through the broken doors to my motorcycle outside. Mounting it, I clipped my backpack in front and noticed the cat jumping over the broken door, coming up to me like this was normal behavior. "No! Bad kitty. You're not coming..." He jumped up onto my legs and swished his tail to smack me in the face, silencing my protests. Maybe it was because he was so desperate to be with me, or maybe I was just desperate for another heartbeat. Either way, I gave in. "Alright, *god*. You can come with me. Fluffy manipulator." Carefully, I picked him up and unzipped my jacket to stuff him inside against my chest before zipping it back up. He wiggled a bit before he settled against me and tucked his head under my chin.

Seems like I've become a crazy cat lady after all.

My motorcycle came to life with a thrust, and kitty and Kitty left the tower behind.

IT TOOK me several hours to find the supplier's location, owing to the fact that the ledger simply specified '*37 miles in that direction, past this old restaurant, and turn when you see a roost of chickens.*' The bleeder clearly had seen no value in writing down street signs or using a compass. If I hadn't already killed him, I might've again just for his vague accounting.

Knowing my value for human life had sunk over the past two decades was enough to sober me. My mother had fought a damn war trying to protect human life. She valued it almost over her own, and now I was shooting bleeders for being stupid. She'd be ashamed of me.

Sniffing, I wiped my face with my gloves and unzipped my jacket to let the kitty out once we'd arrived at our destination. He bounced from the handles to the ground and trotted around to rub against an old stop sign before looking back at me expectantly.

"We're about to go in hot, puss. Could be dangerous," I informed him. He lifted a paw to give it a delicate lick, completely unfazed. Lifting an eyebrow at my furry companion, I checked the chamber in my gun and slipped Artemis back into her holster, giving her a comforting pat for what we were about to face. "Saddle up, puss. It's time to lock and load." I adjusted my vest and started towards the building with the black kitty trotting beside me.

Standing in front of the building, it was hard to tell what this place had been before as all the windows were boarded up and the front had been painted black. Cautiously, I tried the handle on the front door, and it swung open to show several bleeders holding rifles.

They'd been waiting for me.

"Human, drinker, or mutt?" the biggest one demanded, clicking the safety off his gun. Puss stepped past the enemy lines and rubbed against the bleeder's leg. He lifted his boot to lightly shoo the cat away. "Answer before I shoot you between the eyes."

"Rude," I mumbled, casually darting my eyes around to assess my odds if they decided to go postal on me. "No one ever asks my name first. Can't a lady demand a bit of wining and dining?" The bleeder worked his jaw and narrowed his eyes at me. He reminded me so much of the stoic blonde that loved my mother. "Drinker," I answered after a few beats.

The bleeder tightened his hold on his gun, checking behind me for something on the street. "Did you bring sharks with you?"

"Do I look fixed in the head? Of course not." He seemed less certain and waved two fingers for the rest of his group to come out and search the block, just in case. "Can't see sharks being the best thing to bring to a dinner party," I snarked as I watched them. Satisfied I wasn't planning an ambush, the bleeders led me inside before closing the heavy door and slamming a bar across it. Emergency lights came on across the ceiling, lighting up the dirty metal entrance.

"Weapons," the bleeder demanded as his eyes adjusted to the dim light, lowering his gun to hang on his side.

I resisted the urge to scowl at him. "As I've said many times to bleeders much stronger than you, Artemis stays with me."

He looked down and saw the cat at my feet. "Your cat's name is Artemis?"

Rolling my eyes, I lifted my gun from her holster. "The gun, bleeder. I don't name cats."

"On the talk of names, mine is Marcus. Yours?"

I curled my mouth inward with a grimace. He was definitely going to laugh at me. "Kitty." A titter went around the bleeders standing beside me, making me roll my eyes again.

Why did my mom have to give me such an adorable name?

"Kitty with a kitty," one teased. He ended up with my gun in his face before he could giggle again, and Marcus reached up a hand to get between us.

"Now, now. Calm down, kitten," he cautioned. "There'll be no shooting today."

Artemis went back into her holster, but I still leveled the bleeders with my glare. "Call me kitten again and I will make no promises."

"Fair enough." Marcus lifted his hand again and signaled for them to all stand down. "What's your business, drinker?"

I tilted my chin in motion to the rest of the building. "Looking for your boss man. He around?"

"Nearabouts. You lookin' for some red?"

"I'll take my business with your boss, thank you."

Marcus's mouth tilted down, but he nodded wordlessly

and turned to walk down the hallway. I followed, one hand on Artemis in case the bleeders turned on me.

Horror stories had circulated amongst vampires about humans capturing us to become their own personal Night Shadow farms. One vampire and one Lycan in a cage would set a bleeder up for decades.

Puss didn't care if we were being led into an ambush as he followed at my heels like we were off to a picnic with the Queen. Various scents wafted up to me from the slightly damp and poorly lit hallway, but none of them were blood. That boded well. Or it just meant they were good at cleaning up their kills. I couldn't afford to be completely trusting of anyone.

At the end of the hall was a door with two guards, and Marcus nodded at them to open it. They eyed me, a sneer curling on their lips, but they stayed silent. I tapped Artemis with a single finger and grinned as I walked past them.

Inside the room they guarded was a bald man wearing a white suit that had seen better days, but was still presentable enough for guests. He sat at a table eating a steak and potatoes dinner, complete with a glass of wine. I could hardly think with the smell of his food in my head. It had been a very long time since I'd had meat. Blood didn't count. It was too risky to spill blood and build a fire to cook it when there were sharks literally everywhere. They'd be on me faster than it would take to brown the meat.

"Marcus," the boss man said, his nose still tilted towards his plate as he sawed at the steak and brought a bite to his lips. "Bring a chair for our guest." The meat went into his mouth and I felt my own start to water. Marcus brought up a folding chair for me and placed it across his boss at the table, then motioned for me to come forward and sit in it.

Puss waltzed up and jumped into the chair, swishing his tail back and forth.

"Yours?" the boss asked, flicking his fork at the cat. I nodded, trying not to put my hand on Artemis as I often did in tense situations. "Don't suppose you'd sell him to me?"

"Is that what you're eating? Cat?" I shuddered inwardly.

"Buffalo," he answered with a dry laugh. "There's a herd about fifty miles east of here. They've re-populated much of the region. We eat hearty." Hungry and weakened, I couldn't hide my lust over his spread, and he motioned to someone who left the room. "Sit, please." Puss jumped down for me and just as I sat, the other bleeder came back with an identical plate of steak and potatoes that he set in front of me.

I didn't wait for niceties, I took the fork and knife, cut into the meat as daintily as I'd been taught by my mother, and put it to my lips to smear them with grease before taking a delicate bite.

Gods almighty. I had never tasted anything so delicious.

The juices. The flavors. All rolling around my tongue filling me with sensations. He'd salted and seasoned it to perfection. Even Knight would've cried having something this good to eat. I was seriously regretting not taking the time to hunt for meat.

"I'm Morpheus," my dining companion said as he watched me cut another bite and plop it into my mouth.

"Kitty," I offered around my bite, cutting off another piece and shoving it between my lips before my previous bite had been fully chewed.

"Not often we get drinkers here." He lifted his wine glass to his lips and drank of the red liquid. "I suppose you're here for some supply?" Not wanting to stop eating, I reached for the baggie in my back pocket and tossed it onto the table in front of me. "Ahh. You already have some."

"I need to know where you got it. Whose blood it is." Lifting my bag off my shoulders, I pulled out the ledger and laid it beside the baggie. "I got it from a bleeder."

"Hmm," Morpheus said, taking the ledger and opening it. "This belongs to Andrew." He waited a breath and looked up to catch my gaze. "Belonged..." It ended almost as a question.

My fingers tightened on my fork and I slowly worked my jaw to chew the meat in my mouth. I'd have felt sheepish if I actually cared about it, but I had no idea if Morpheus would be pissed at me for killing his friend. "He called me girlie."

"A mistake I will not repeat," Morpheus said with a slight grin, apparently not caring in the slightest about me killing the bleeder. "I gave Andrew a new supply three months ago. It came from Salvation. I don't know more than that, I'm sorry."

I speared a potato with my fork and bit into it with my fangs, just so my dinner companion was reminded of what I was capable of. "Salvation? What's that?"

"The last human city, so they say. Drinkers, mutts, and humans living together." He sipped his wine again and adjusted one of the rings on his fingers. A twitch if I ever saw one. Studying him carefully, I took another bite. He was hiding something.

"Any idea where it's located?"

He tilted his head in a shrug. "Can't rightly say."

My eyes flicked cautiously to Marcus and the other bleeders standing around us. "You must have some idea."

"It's not exactly a place I'd want to go to," he explained, his shoulders relaxing slightly, but not enough to bring my guard down.

Leaning back in my chair so he wouldn't be tipped off that I was suspicious of him, I brought another potato to my fangs and tore into it. "Too many drinkers for your taste, I'm guessing?"

With a distant look in his eyes, he folded his hands on his belly, making my pulse shoot off so rapidly I was glad he couldn't hear it. "There's a woman there. We've heard stories about her. She commands the vampires with a single word. Her power over them keeps them in line, makes them ignore their carnal instincts of destruction so they can work with the humans."

Intrigued, I sat up, my food forgotten. "Is there a name attached to this woman?"

Morpheus grinned at me, like a ten-year-old telling a ghost story. "They call her the Countess."

The name sent a shiver up my spine. Lords almighty. It had to be her.

I stood, my chair skidding on the concrete floor. "Thank you for the meal and the information. I'll be on my way."

"You may just want to rethink that part," Morpheus cautioned. Marcus had snuck up to me, grabbing Artemis before I could stop him, even with my enhanced speed.

"There's another tale I've heard, much more interesting than the Countess," Morpheus said as he stood. "A tale about a black haired purple eyed girl whose blood makes the best Night Shadow on the planet. Know anyone like that?" His mouth rose in a sickening grin and the bleeders lifted their guns at me.

My fangs dropped, and I flung my hands out as my nails grew into claws. "You're a fool if you think you can capture me."

He laughed at me again and took a gun from his belt, pointed it at me with wasted confidence. "I doubt that, girlie."

Then he fired.

5

HE'LL COME BACK

DREYA

"Darling, you look pale."

I smiled, showing several of my perfect teeth. "Darius, that joke started getting old when we were still in high school."

My boyfriend leaned in to kiss me, his aura bathed in the colors pink and yellow, and then he straightened to look out at the sunset with me. I looped my arm in his and leaned my head against his shoulder, watching the blue sky be engulfed with shades of red and orange. We stood on the tallest building in Salvation, the clock tower where both of our families lived.

"Your mother is going to see red if I keep you out any later," Darius warned as he leaned in for another kiss. And another. And another, until I was breathless against him. His short, brown curls were soft under my fingers and I tugged on them to get him closer to me, standing on my tip-toes. The scent of his human blood was a perfume that swirled around me in temptation, but just as I didn't allow Darius to go further than kisses, I also would never drink from him. I pulled away after another sweet kiss and planted my feet on the floor.

"Let's go. Mother can be a bit of a pill." We grinned and left the balcony hand in hand. The clockwork gears moved beside us as we went down the stairs and stopped at the fifth-floor landing for another kiss.

"Good night, Dreya." Darius planted a soft kiss on my nose and stroked my cheek, staring into my blue eyes like he was looking at a priceless piece of art. "I could stand here for an eternity, just waiting for one more kiss."

"And I think you're a sweet-talker who likes goading my parents," I chided with a smile.

Sighing, he leaned into the stairwell wall, still holding my hand. "You're nineteen. Almost twenty. And you still have all these ridiculous restrictions on yourself. You're an adult, Dreya."

I felt like sighing too, but I held it in with practiced patience and tucked a strand of my blonde hair behind my ear. "Darius, you know it's different for us. I'm a vampire. We mature slowly. It takes decades. My sister was still acting like a moody teenager at thirty. I suspect the same will be true for me." I wiggled our clasped hands. "Let's not fight, hmm?" He smiled when he saw an answering grin on my face.

Pushing away from the wall, Darius came to clasp my face

between his hands. "Dinner tomorrow at my place?" I nodded happily and he gave me another peck on my nose. "Night. For real this time." I finger waved at him and slipped out of the stairwell and onto the hallway, tiptoeing my way down to my bedroom door. Quietly, I opened it and slipped inside, making sure to keep the doorknob twisted until it was fully closed so it wouldn't make a sound.

"Hi."

"*Gods,*" I swore, putting a hand to my chest. Sitting on my bed was my mother, her arms crossed over her nightgown and her purple eyes staring me down. "I'm sorry I was out so late, mother."

She rolled her eyes. "Dreya, you're not five. You don't have a bedtime." Her gaze scanned me, and I knew she was feeling my power levels, just in case I'd gotten a little fang happy with Darius.

"I didn't drink from him," I told her as I put my bag down onto my desk

"You'd better not have. You know I don't give two shakes if you do, but the humans will throw you in prison before you can say, '*verisimilitude.*'" Her face softened and she shut her eyes with a sigh. "I'm sorry. You know I don't like being snappy."

With her walls down, I reached out with my power. Her aura was a deep, inky blue, and it brought a frown to my face. "You're sad. You're sad because Kitty and Jason are still missing. And father is gone."

Her lip trembled and she looked away. She stared out my

window as if it held secrets she longed to know. "Every year it gets harder."

I stepped across my carpet and sat next to her on my comforter. "I know." We both looked out and I could still see a hint of the sunset between the buildings of Salvation. "I remember his face. His eyes." She reached between us to take my hand and her aura fluttered with a slight pink underneath the blue. "He'll come back. I know he will. I feel it. One day those eyes will be looking at you again."

She shuddered as if she could actually be cold and her aura shifted to a blank color. She was good at hiding herself. "The things that I hate is that..." She swallowed. "I never told him how much I loved him. And now maybe... maybe I'll never get the chance."

"He knew, mother. Both of them know how much you love them. When you're with dad, you're the brightest yellow and pink I've ever seen in my life, second only to father's, if it could ever be brighter. Which I doubt."

Her eyes found mine when she turned her head. "What were my colors like with your father?"

I smiled and recalled the last day we'd seen him. A day of sadness and regret. My smile fell, but I searched through and found her color, that last moment when she met his eyes before he was taken away. "Your second brightest pink. Only a twinge dimmer than the first."

Mother leaned back on her hands and stared up at my ceiling with the glow in the dark stars dad had stuck on when I was little. "Of all the powers my kids could get, yours had to be reading auras. You'll never understand how weird it was to have a two-year-old pointing at me yelling, '*Pink! Pink!*'" We giggled at the memory we both had.

"You're almost always pink," I reminded her. "When you're not blue."

Her smile fell again and she sat up to stand. "Seems I'm blue most of the time now. A perfect fixture on my aura." It was true, but I didn't want her to know it for certain.

"He'll come back," I said again firmly.

Her eyebrows curled in thought and she looked back at me. "They'll kill him if he does." Blue gained ground and surrounded her, a blue so deep I feared I would be sucked into it. I shivered this time and watched her leave, shutting my door behind her.

6

THE PRISONER

KITTY

Being shot was all sorts of fun. Being grossly outnumbered, not so much. By the time I'd finished with those bleeders, I was riddled with holes in my perfect skin. Stupid bleeders had vampire bullets. That was playing dirty. Puss had taken the hint and ran out the door behind where Morpheus lay on the floor, his body dripping blood from several places. He was no longer drawing enough breath to call me girlie.

"Puss?" I called into the open doorway as I sheathed Artemis in my belt. My palm left a bloodied handprint on the door when I pushed on it and stuck my head into the second hallway. The black cat was halfway down it, stopped at something. He looked back where I stood and meowed at me. "What? Is it catnip?"

Meow.

"Fine. Better not be catnip, just telling you that now." I entered the hallway and clomped down to where the cat sat next to an open door and immediately recoiled in shock. Inside the room was a passed out Lycan, and by the looks of him, he was in bad shape. I said a few choice words, describing exactly what I thought about the bleeders I'd just massacred, with enough venom I had to spit onto the floor. I felt no shame about ridding the earth of them, now that I knew what they'd been hiding.

Pushing my senses out, I smelled no other bodies here, though I did smell vampire blood in the room beside this one. Carefully, I walked inside to where the Lycan lay on the carpet. He had bruises on bruises, and caked on blood in so many places, I wasn't sure what color his skin was. His dark hair had been shorn off with small patches here and there where they'd missed spots. A chain led to a collar around his neck, one with spikes that were designed to kill him if he shifted into a wolf.

More choice words spilled out of my mouth, and I wished I'd killed the bleeders slowly, and with enough pain that they begged for mercy.

Puss came in and rubbed past my boots to the Lycan where he stopped and simply stared on. Was he concerned? Gods. Of course he wasn't. He was a *cat*.

Wiping tears from my cheeks, I straightened my spine. "Stay with him. I'll be back." I left them there to find where Morpheus had kept his records and his stash. There was a safe in a small room down the hall, and of course, I easily tore the door off. The safe held what I needed, and I put it inside my backpack before coming back to the Lycan. I ripped the collar off him and threw it at the room's only window so hard, it broke the glass and sailed outside. "Heads up," I cautioned to no one, and carefully picked up the boy.

Both Kitties walked down the hall, past the worthless corpses, and back outside to where I'd left my motorcycle. Using some rope I carried with me, I tied the Lycan to me, chest to chest, so he wouldn't go flying off my ride when he woke up. Despite his protests, I stuffed Puss into my backpack.

With both passengers secured, I pumped the throttle, my bike roared to life, and I sped off down the empty street, leaving the corpses to become shark bait.

WITH THE EXTRA weight of the Lycan, I didn't want to travel very far. I found an old supermarket that hadn't been entirely picked clean of food and brought us all inside, bike included, before barricading the door. The store's florescent lights barely functioned after so long, but a few still worked, probably from solar panels on the roof. After finding the employee break room couch still intact, I placed the Lycan on top of it. Puss took the opportunity to lay right across the Lycan's collarbone.

"Shoo," I said to him, though I had a feeling he would ignore me.

He did.

I sighed and rolled my eyes, wondering why I'd allowed this flea bag to come along with me.

Finally slowing down after the fact, the pain of the bullets inside me was starting to twinge. I'd have to remove all of them and then feed on a few sharks to recover. They'd come for the feast I just left them, it just depended on how far away they were, and I had a feeling those bleeders kept their city clean of the beasts. If I played my cards right, I'd get a full belly of shark blood before the week was over.

I'd just removed my jacket when the Lycan burst awake, shouting and throwing Puss from him, causing a very loud cat roar when he hit the carpet feet down. I held up a bloodied hand to the Lycan, which wasn't the best method to calm him down.

"You're safe, you're safe," I repeated several times as he jumped up from the couch, frantic in his haste to get away from me. He found a corner and backed into it with his hands up to protect his face.

"You stay there, drinker!" he shouted at me. His deep, brown eyes spotted my gun and his pulse shot up even more. "I'll kill you if you try to drink my blood!"

"Wasn't gonna," I assured him, trying not to wrinkle my nose at the thought of his blood in my mouth. "I only drink vampire blood."

That threw him, and he lowered his hands, his pulse slowing. "What kind of vampire only drinks vampire blood?"

Slowly, I lifted Artemis from my holster and tossed her

onto the couch, further reducing his heart rate. "The special kind. The kind that saves your life and kills all the *cabrón*[1] bleeders that held you captive. Mind you, I didn't know you were there when I killed them. But I would've just the same if I had." The Lycan's eyes moved to where Artemis lay and I saw his brain turning, wondering if he could get to it before I could. Unlikely, but then again, a bleeder had disarmed me not an hour earlier. "I'm Kitty. That's my name, I'm not talking about the cat. He doesn't have a name."

With his heart almost at a normal rhythm, he stopped eyeing the gun in panic and looked me over, studying the woman who'd saved him from the bleeders. Was I someone he could trust? He seemed to decide I was because his pinched mouth relaxed. "I'm Cody. And I'm pretty sure only psychopaths don't name their pets."

"Hey," I complained loudly. "That is an insult to all the psychopaths out there. Besides, I named my gun. Does that count?"

"No."

Screw you, wolf boy.

"How long did they have you?" He shrugged and looked away, everything they'd done still too fresh in his mind. "There's some food downstairs. Let's go grab some. I think we both need a snack." I chomped my teeth together in mock warning and he didn't find it as amusing as I did. Giving me a wide berth, he followed me downstairs and we left Artemis on the couch.

While Cody searched through the food I'd smelled, I

found a bottle of motor oil in an aisle that had the fresh odor of rat pee and brought it over to my cycle by the barricaded doors. I was tipping it into the oil chamber when Cody came over with two cans. One was baked beans and the other alphabet soup.

"There's a can opener in my bag." I motioned with my chin towards it and tossed the motor oil bottle when it was empty, screwing the oil cap back on.

"That's a sweet ride," Cody complimented as he sat down and opened the cans. "Solar powered?" I nodded, cautiously closing the distance between us to sit in front of him. Puss came and sat beside me, completing the circle. Cody handed me one of the cans, the alphabet soup one, and I scooped out a bit to put on the floor for the cat. He dug in with gusto and I started on the rest of it. It wasn't gourmet, but it filled my stomach, and that was nice considering I rarely ate full meals. I hadn't even had a chance to finish the steak Morpheus gave me before shooting them all up and ruining it.

"Your folks nearby?" I asked him. I knew I was hitting a nerve when he looked away, but he swallowed and took a scoop of baked beans to his mouth.

"They're a ways. Doesn't make much sense to live near drug dealers. They'll take your trade and then steal your kids." He looked down, his mind miles away.

"Hey," I said, bringing him out of it for a moment. "We're not talking about that. I just want to know where I can take you where you'll be safe."

"The path is marked. I can find home again."

I got up and felt the tug of my torn skin under the bullets. They needed to come out. "Gonna clean up. I suggest you do the same." He nodded, and I disappeared into the women's bathroom. Thankfully one of the lights in there was working with very few flickers.

I removed my jacket, shirt, and pants before accessing my injuries, and not having Artemis made me feel more naked than I currently was. The bullets on my person numbered nine, a much lower number than I expected given how much pain I was feeling. I reached two fingers into the first hole and pain sliced through me as I grabbed hold of the bullet and yanked it out, tossing it into the porcelain sink. The rest followed, and I grabbed a rag from my backpack to wet under the faucet before running it over my skin to catch all the red.

So much red. And this time, all of it mine. Well. Most.

Finished cleaning myself, I ran my hair under the faucet as much as I could and shook out the curls as they rained droplets over the floor. The bullet holes were still there since I was so low on blood, mottled dots on my skin. I dressed again and left, following Cody's scent to the break room. He had cleaned up as much as he could considering most of the color dotting his dark skin was pure bruise. He'd even taken a razor to his hair and now it was all one length. Artemis was still on the couch where I'd left her with Puss curled up on top of her barrel. I retrieved the gun and took it with me to a second more lumpy couch in the room where I fell asleep almost instantly.

7

ICY BLUES

KITTY

The next morning, I found out just what 'marked' meant.

Dog pee.

After being captured by the bleeders, Cody had marked a trail whenever he could, *gross*, and his keen senses could still pick it up. He'd only been with them for a few weeks and rain had been scarce, so it hadn't been washed away. Lucky for us.

Still. Following a trail of pee was a level of disgusting I never wanted to reach. And yet, here we were, Cody with his nose very close to a tree, Puss zipped up in my jacket, and me waiting atop my cycle. Satisfied, Cody came back and mounted behind me, slipping his hands around my middle as I kicked off and started the engine.

We sped off away from the trees and out to the plains.

The land stretched out before us like a blanket and I felt Cody tapping on my shoulder to get my attention. Beside us was a herd of elephants, eating grass and bathing themselves in a small water tank. They watched us drive by, but thankfully they stayed put and didn't charge. One of the babies swung his trunk at us and roared a tiny roar.

"They're beautiful!" Cody hooted into my ear. Even I could find a smile for the creatures. Past them, we stopped again to find the trail and kept going down the road. It was late afternoon when Cody came back from sniffing with a smile on his face. "We're close," he pronounced before hopping up behind me. The knowledge sent me faster through the fields until Cody started directing me down some hidden paths and the plains turned into a forest.

Deep inside it, past countless trees and enough pee odor to make my nose curl, we came upon a small encampment. Trailers, vans, a school bus, all parked in a semi-circle around a brick and mortar campfire. I smelled Lycans and humans. And maybe... a hint of vampires? It was hard to tell. The dog smell hid our scent well. Overpowering as well was the scent of cooking meat, and my stomach growled in response.

As soon as the campers saw us, they all brought out their guns in warning, and almost as quickly dropped them when they saw Cody behind me. Several of them shouted his name, and he started running towards them as soon as I stopped my bike, grabbing several of his kin in his arms. The tallest Lycan there, the Alpha, still had his gun in his hand as he regarded me and stepped closer. His head twisted to the side in thought and he looked at me like he'd seen a ghost. I almost echoed the look because his scent was familiar to me.

"Lisbeth?" Of course they knew her. She was a household name amongst vampires and Lycans after the turned war.

I stepped off my bike and put the kick stand up. "Close. I'm her daughter. Kitty."

"You look just like her. Except for the—"

"—eyes," I finished for him with a knowing grin. It was what everyone said. "I'm surprised you remember her. Were you part of our village?" His face was equally familiar, but I couldn't quite place it. Maybe my memories were slow because of how hungry I was for blood.

"I'm Simon, I don't know if you remember me," he answered just as Cody came to hug him. "Thank you for returning my son."

"Holy dragon bogies," I whispered under my breath. Simon, the little kid my mom had saved was all grown up. And now I'd just saved his kid. Talk about a full circle. "You're so big! And you have kids!"

He laughed and brought me in for a hug. "You're big too, squirt! You were just a baby last time I saw you! How did you even remember me?"

I tapped a finger to my head and grinned. "Vamp memory. I remember everything. *Everything.*"

His face fell when he saw the unhealed bullet holes on my neck. "Cody, go find the vampires. They're hunting to the south. Shouldn't be far." Cody ran off and I watched him with the fading protective instinct I'd gained after merely one day together. "Where'd you find him?" Simon asked, studying me carefully with his brown eyes.

I unzipped my jacket and let Puss out. He hopped down and ran to the fire pit to find out where the meat smell was coming from. "Drug den. They were using him to make Night Shadow."

Simon's jaw tensed and his hands formed fists at his sides, his wolf straining to come out. "They dead?"

Nodding, I put a hand to Artemis and pat her in a comforting gesture. "They met an untimely end, for sure. I saw to that."

Simon let out a dry chuckle at me. "You're so like her. It's unreal."

Hope bubbled up inside me and I looked around, sniffing the scents for any I recognized. The hope burst when I couldn't find her smell but I kept my face blank. "Is my mom here?"

"No, no. She's not here. I was referring to someone else."

Before I could ask what he meant, Cody shouted as he came back into view amongst the tree trunks. He waved and motioned to the two men beside him, carrying a buck between them.

"No *way*," I swore under my breath.

One of the men was unknown to me, but the other restored my optimism. When he saw my face, I knew he thought I was her, if only for a brief moment, because he looked as if all the sunlight in the world was finally back over the horizon. His features fell when he realized who I was, and he was back to that stoic iciness that I knew. As he reached me, I tossed my hair back and nodded to him.

"Hello, Arthur."

8

NO REALLY, HE'LL COME BACK

DREYA

*I*t was hard to sleep after seeing mother so upset, especially knowing I'd caused some of it.

I knew, I *knew* my father would come back. I knew it with as much certainty as I knew the sun would rise in the morning and set in the evening. Even so, I wished my clarity had given me some insight as to what had happened to my siblings. Jason and Kitty were still missing after twenty long years, my entire life. It weighed on both my parents, even father before he'd been sent away. I felt the weight of the loss as well, despite having never met the rest of my family. I knew all about every single one of them, so much so I liked to believe that when the day came that they stood before me, I'd know instantly that it was them.

Kitty. Jason. Balthazar. Grandmother Anastasia.

I fell asleep with them all in my head and wished I could dream a dream that led them back to us.

The next morning, I entered the large living room across the hall from my room to see my dad making breakfast on our little stove, wearing mother's apron with his long hair up in a man bun. He turned and an unruly shank of his black locks fell out of the bun and into his eyes. He was all pink this morning. Dad was good at blocking out bad emotions and making only the good ones shine through.

"Hey, kiddo! Sleep well? Darius keeping his hands to himself?" I glared at him jokingly as I sat at the small table between the sofa and the fridge. If I leaned my chair back just right, it caught on the sofa, giving me a perfect lounge angle. I did so and folded my hands over my flat belly as I smelled the blueberry pancakes he was making.

"Where'd you get blueberries, dad? Is it a special occasion?" At my words, his aura shimmered with some gray before the pink replaced it. Ahh. So the blueberries weren't just because. He was trying to cheer mother up. "She asleep?"

"She's having a bad day, love." He flipped a pancake and stirred the batter a little before adding another to the griddle.

"I can see what really bothers her when she's thinking about him," I told dad, watching him purposefully face away from me.

"Attempting to unravel the mystery that is your mother is a daring feat, Dreya." He finally faced me, and I saw streaks on his deep brown skin where he'd been crying and hadn't washed them away. "I've been married to her for fifty-five years and I still find myself surprised sometimes."

Patting across the kitchen tiles, he put a plate in front of me stacked with blueberry pancakes, set one down for him, and took a tray from the counter over to the closed door on the right side of the kitchen where their bedroom was. I took my fork and watched him knock on the door, wait for her response, then he stepped into the room and came back without the tray. Digging into my breakfast, I took a bite of the pancake and savored the rare taste of the fresh blueberries. Dad sat across from me and started eating his too.

"Dreya," he started, hesitating over his plate. "You know I don't parent you very often. Neither of us do. But..." He trailed off and reached out a hand for me. I took it and his colors shifted into a rainbow of emotions. "Please don't tell your mother that Arthur is coming back. She can't handle it. I know you were just trying to help, but please don't say things like that."

A very rare emotion rumbled through me and I narrowed my eyes at the man I called dad. "I wasn't trying to comfort her. I know he's coming back. I may see auras, but I also sense things. And I've known since the day he was sent away that he would return."

"You were seven, Dreya."

"Knight," mother said, interrupting us as she appeared at their bedroom door. Dad's spine straightened and he shut his eyes, knowing she'd heard him. All around her, the blue started giving way to pink, and I was almost blinded by the sight of it. I had to look away, blinking several times.

"Geez, mom. You're so bright. It's like the fourth of July. I can't see." I heard her come into the room, set her tray onto the table, and put her arms around Dad, kissing him somewhere. I opened my eyes to see her leaning against his back, her head on top of his and his hands clutching hers across his chest. They had a look on their faces that meant they were communicating telepathically, a skill I very much envied. She smiled and kissed him on his long, dark hair. With focus, I turned down the volume of my powers and their sunlight auras dimmed down to a thin line around them.

"I'm sorry, Dreya," dad said as mother sat down beside him.

It took me only a second to smile at him, and I imagined my colors were bright pink too. "As you said, you don't parent me. Why start now?"

"Yeah. All that snark. Totally yours, my love," he said to mother.

"Please. Arthur could snark with the best of them." She picked up her fork and cut into her stack of pancakes. Her hand shook slightly, but she put a few pieces of it into her mouth.

She was wrong. So wrong.

Father would come back. I knew it.

I LEFT the pink lovebirds to their business and exited the clock tower we called home out onto the city streets of Salvation. Human guards stood here and there with their vampire piercing bullets, and I chose to nod to them with a smile as I passed each one, pretending their sole purpose wasn't to shoot my people.

Even in the market, the guards remained on their silent vigil, but I ignored them this time. Salvation ran on ration credits. Every month, we were all given a book of ration coupons, as was done many years before during war time. One for eggs, one for bread, and so on. I had my coupon book ready to get something hot for breakfast before I had to journey to the edge of town for my daily blood ration.

Once I'd reached the food stand I wanted, one with steaming fresh cheese bread, I tore out one of my fresh meal coupons and waited in line behind several humans. When it was my turn, I smiled at the woman serving the food and presented my coupon, but instead of smiling back, she sneered at me and wrapped up a small loaf of the cheese bread, roughly pressing it into my hands. Still, using that practiced patience, I nodded my head to her in thanks and headed on my way.

The bread was stale and moldy, I discovered. The humans here mostly tolerated us, but there were some that blamed this all on vampires. To be fair, we did have a hand in it, but it wasn't our fault. Mother had even risked imprisonment and exile to warn humans about the drones when the mass turning began. Her help had saved thousands of lives. It didn't matter much when humans believed their loved ones were still lost to them, even if the only difference was they preferred blood over steak.

A few of the city's dogs roamed the streets and I tossed bits of the moldy bread to them as I struggled to find edible parts for myself. By the time I reached my destination, I'd eaten enough to fill my stomach, and the dogs' as well. When the dogs stopped to sniff the ground, they ran in the other direction, away from the building I had to go inside.

Two guards stood at the door, a vampire and a Lycan. Since both species had a vested interest in the building's occupants, we kept them safe with one of our own. Both guards were known to me, but I could hardly call them friends. I flipped to the back of my coupon book and tore out one sheet to hand over. The vampire took it and rapped on the door with his knuckles before it opened, and I stepped inside.

I'll say right now that this was my least favorite part of town. Mother and Darius hated that I had to go there, but I was not permitted otherwise. Maybe if Darius and I were married, things would be different. I doubted, but I could dream at least.

The room I stepped into had several scents attached, and most were ones I didn't want inside my nose. To remedy that, there was incense burning in every corner for those with sensitive senses. The girls inside the room knew my face and several got up from their lounges to greet me.

"Dreya, you're looking lovely today," one said in a syrupy voice. She draped herself over a column near the door and breathed heavily. She was strung out, hyped up on Night Shadow. Most of them were.

The head girl gave me a hug when she approached and kissed me on my temple. "Governor Hendrix continues to be a cruel man, making a sweet flower like you come to this hell hole."

"But his son is easy on the eyes," the strung-out girl noted with a grin. The girls went by stage names, and as their real names were unknown to me, I never referred to them by a façade. They were simply nameless girls. "Tempted to use one of those coupons in the back of your book, Dreya?" She winked with her heavily mascaraed eye and her equally heavily dilated pupils.

I burned those coupons every time I got a new book.

"No thank you," I said, smiling even though I didn't feel it. "Just my ration." The head girl took my hand and walked me to the designated side room, closing the door. This room only smelled like blood, and I welcomed the change.

"I'm sorry about the girls," the head girl fussed as she sat down on the sofa. I joined her and picked up her arm to inspect the skin there. It had several bite marks already, fresh ones.

"You've already given today," I noted, dropping her arm.

She held it back up for me, insisting. "You can't drink from the girls with Night Shadow in their system, your mother would have my hide. I'm always available for a clean drink, I don't mind giving extra."

With a sigh, I took her wrist again and picked a spot of skin that wasn't bruised or pink from the bites, and brought it to my lips to sink my teeth in. I swallowed a few mouthfuls of the life-giving liquid, nowhere near how much I really needed, and pulled away from her, licking the spot clean before I dropped her arm.

"Mmm," she let out a sigh. "That wasn't enough for you."

Silencing her protests, I leaned in and kissed her on her sweaty forehead. "It was all you could spare." I searched and found a blanket on the floor to drape over her so she could rest from the blood loss.

WAITING for me outside the building was my friend, Thomas, another Born vampire. Dressed in camo, his brown hair was arranged in a messy look and his green eyes looked like crisp leaves. He nodded to the guards outside the door and turned as I joined him up the path.

"I'm surprised your boyfriend doesn't pitch a fit over you having to drink here every day," Thomas mentioned, as if he hadn't said it before. Twenty-three times in the past year, my perfect memory recalled. The fact that he always mentioned my boyfriend along with the complaint spoke volumes.

Practiced patience.

A smile touched my lips, and I tried to keep my tone even. "A small sacrifice to keep the peace. So my mother says."

Thomas shrugged and looked away, silent for once. We passed through the market again and went past the clock tower to the back of town where Thomas signed us out at the guard tower. The official record said we were leaving to hunt for meat to bring back to the humans, a task many of the vampires and Lycans took part in daily. While Thomas did in fact find something to bring back for food, that's not what I did during our trips out of the city. It was our secret, mine and his. No one else knew, not even my parents.

We walked past the fence that gave us safety from all the human turned drones, down the shoe trodden road we'd carved over the years. Thomas remained silent, thoughtful, and I didn't like it at all. We had an easy friendship, built on years of spending time together during school, and now that we were graduated, this trip every few weeks was the only time I saw him. I missed the times when words came easy between us. The times before Darius.

Our journey took us far from the city, so far I felt the familiar anxiety that came with being away from my family. Maybe I was afraid if I went too far, I'd return and they wouldn't be there. They'd be gone like father. My feet stilled, and I stopped on the road before we'd reached our destination. Thomas came up beside me and held out his hand for me to take, his dusty fingertips peeking out from his half-gloves.

"They'll be fine," he said gently, his voice deep and soothing, and I ignored the loving pink that came like a beautiful halo above his head. He knew me so well even though we spent so little time together now. Slowly, I brought my hand out and slipped my fingers between his, sparking a shiver up my spine.

Warmth spread over me, and in the midst of my sadness and anxiety, I regretted for one second the path I'd chosen, the path that took me away from Thomas. And then the second passed and I let go of his hand.

"Let's go, we'll be late getting back," I said, looking away. Thomas dropped his hand and sighed, then he turned on his heel and kept walking down the road. I followed behind, keeping my gaze on the back of his boots.

Soon, far too soon, we reached the building hidden behind a barrier of trees and bushes. Thomas brought out one of his knives and pressed it into my hands.

"I'll be back in a few hours. If I'm not back by then—"

"Go back on my own so I won't get in trouble," I finished. He nodded at me, reached out to squeeze my shoulder, and left the way we'd come. With his fading smell behind me, I walked up to the door and knocked three times. It opened and the scent of fresh bread came to me, releasing the tension in my shoulders.

"Lucas!" Clara exclaimed at the sight of me. "Dreya is here!"

9

PLANS IN MOTION

KITTY

"Kitty," Arthur said in greeting when the three reached me and dropped their kill on the forest floor. His short, blonde hair was in that perfect rugged style, and his icy blue eyes seemed more distant than I remembered. His voice still had that rough edge to it, as rough as his own edges. I felt like apologizing for making him think even for a second that I was my mom, but he would've just ignored it. "This is Dominic." He gestured to the other vampire, an also ruggedly blonde man who tipped his chin to me. He smiled and I saw his eyes were two different colors. One was blue and the other brown, an anomaly similar to my own. My wonky iris kinsmen. It was weird to feel a connection to him, but there it was.

"Hello, Kitty," he said in a slight accent. Australian? "Arthur has told me a lot about you." He held out a hand for me to shake, and I did so, only to feel a shock of electricity race up my arm at the touch of his fingers, the way I'd always reacted when Thalia touched me.

"I'm surprised he stopped talking about my mom long enough to mention me," I snarked, throwing Arthur a saucy grin. He gave me a look I knew was him rolling his eyes in his silent way.

Arthur and Dom skinned the deer, and we sat around the fire pit as the sun started setting, the deer meat cooking on a spit that Dom slowly turned. Arthur passed around some fresh cornbread and sat across the fire from me, next to one of the Lycan females. Maybe they were more than friends, considering how she smiled at him. I couldn't say why, but seeing them sitting together like that made my teeth curl. I bit into the sweet cornbread and tried to focus on something other than the vampire sitting across from me.

"I'd love to hear what you've been up to, Kitty," Arthur said with a slight smile. He was *smiling* now. Dude followed my mom like a lovesick pony my entire life and he was happier without her. *Ass.*

"I too would like to hear what you've been up to, *Arthur*," I mimicked, giving a hard look to both him and the Lycan female. Arthur's smile fell and he returned to the icy blankness.

"I asked first," he retorted evenly. I leaned back and could swear I heard Dom snickering from the spit handle.

"Well, I started out with my team in Canada twenty years ago. We stayed together after everything went dark." The fire popped and I glanced at Dom, still cranking the spit. He had his head half turned towards my voice with his eyes still focused on the meat. "Every so often we'd find more vampires, and we had a sizable coven before..." I looked down at the fire and I could see it all before me, that day that had changed everything.

The screaming. The blood. And Thalia...

"Shark attack?" Dominic guessed, and I nodded, my eyes still on the fire.

"I was the sole survivor, because I was the only one who could drink from the sharks. The rest... we didn't have any humans nearby, so they bled out. I left Canada and I came down here, trying to find Jason. When that didn't work, I focused on finding Lisbeth."

"That's why you were in the Night Shadow den?" Simon asked, having stayed silent until then like the rest of the Lycans. Arthur's eyebrows lifted before his entire face dropped in a scowl, making sure I knew just how he disapproved of me messing with drugs. I made my face as *you're not my dad* as possible.

"Finding you is the closest I've come to her in twenty years. I take it you know where she is?" He nodded once, and I could've cried with the relief that flooded all over my body. I sighed and my voice cracked with the sound. Swiping a hand over my eyes, I focused up at the stars. "Is Jason with her?"

"No." The relief crashed down to earth like a comet and more tears came for a different reason. Several curse words escaped my lips before I could stop them. Finding my mom was perfect. My goal for so long, yes. But knowing Jason was still lost made me feel even more empty.

"We don't know where he is," Arthur continued, silencing my next question. He looked as grave as I felt, and though it was odd, I felt a kinship with him over the crackling fire.

I swiped my nose again. "Can you take me to her?"

Arthur pressed his lips into a thin line and he focused on the fire like I had, lost in thought. "That would be difficult."

"I'm sensing a really long backstory. Can you give me the cliffs notes?"

He glared at me. "I put up with your mom's sass because I care about her. You, I'd much rather put in time out."

"Je-*sus*, cowboy. You've gotten grumpy in your old age." As much as I hated his attitude, I enjoyed getting under his skin. I'd never seen him this way.

"Kitty," he admonished with a snap. "Stop being such a twit."

"Rawr," I mimed a cat noise with my claws out. He continued glaring at me, so I rolled my eyes. "Fine, I'm sorry. Tell me what happened."

Arthur pierced me with his icy stare, but he continued his tale of woe. "Lisbeth and I had a child together."

What.

I was certain my eyes were the size of saucers when I asked, "Is Knight dead?" And though I would've never expected it, despite my desire to reconcile with him, my stomach churned at the thought of Knight gone.

Arthur looked away and I felt sick enough that I worried

my lunch might come back up. "No, he's not dead. At least I don't think. It was before the drones came." Before the world ended then, before we'd all been separated.

"And I was never told because..." I let it hang off, flipping my palm up, waiting for him to explain.

"It was one attempt, so we hadn't had the chance of telling you and Jason because we didn't know if it had worked yet."

"So you and she..." I motioned with my fingers and he scowled at me so deeply I felt like my head would explode.

"It was a clinical procedure. There was nothing physical between us. There hasn't been since before you were born." Giving him a 'whatever' motion, he continued like I hadn't interrupted. "After the press conference, we escaped from the newly turned drones, and that's when Knight and I discovered that Lisbeth was already pregnant. We stayed hidden during her pregnancy and only came out once the baby was strong enough to be on the road. We bounced from place to place for a few years until we found Salvation. The town, I mean."

Dom stood up and started cutting off pieces of the deer which Simon helped pass around while Arthur continued.

"It seemed a good place to be. We were safe from the drones, and all the humans wanted from us was for others of our kind to help protect them. And then..." He took his plate from Simon, and I wanted to backhand him for stopping. "One night something happened." He took a bite of his meat and seemed finished with his story.

"*What?* What happened?" Okay, now he deserved to be back handed, stopping in the middle of the story like that.

Storyteller he was not. Thankfully, he swallowed and went on before I had a chance to stab him.

"I'm not entirely sure what happened. One minute everything was fine, and then Lisbeth was acting off, saying we had to leave. We got to the edge of the city before the humans stopped us. That night, Lisbeth was on Night Shadow, and it's illegal to consume in Salvation, except for the designated humans vampires feed from. I lied and said I'd given it to her, and they threw me out for it."

"That seems pretty straightforward, bro. Why are you not sure what happened exactly?" I took a bite of the deer meat when Simon handed me my plate, and gods, it tasted amazing. Dom hadn't just turned the handle, he'd been adding salt and a few spices to it as it cooked. I might have to keep him around.

Arthur sighed and stared into the fire again. "She never took Night Shadow. I swear she'd never touched the stuff. I know what it looks like, and she was fine until the humans found us. One of them shoved a flashlight into her face and when she turned around, her pupils were dilated, and she was babbling about shiny unicorns."

"Sounds like Night Shadow," I commented dryly, wiping a greasy hand on my pants. "So you just left her there?"

Arthur glared again, because his face only knew how to make two expressions total. "If it was that simple, I wouldn't be here."

"Salvation is a fortress," Dominic said, his fingers covered in meat juices. He started popping them into his mouth to lick them clean like a cat. Speaking of cats: where was Puss?

"We've been planning, waiting for the right moment, for many years. If this is done incorrectly, it will all be for nothing."

"So we're busting them out? Sounds like fun."

"No," Arthur said, shaking his head. "There's more than a hundred of us in there with the humans, not just our family. If we go in and only take our family, we don't know what will happen to everyone else."

Our family.

"And you're convinced this town is bad news?"

"I'm not sure. All I know is something happened that night, and I don't know what. It could be safe now. We won't know until we're inside."

I looked back at Arthur's icy blues. "I'm in."

VISIONS

KITTY

We finished the deer off, with the Lycans eating all the bones as dessert —eww—, before turning in for the night with the promise of beginning our plan in the morning. I put up my little tent and went in search of Puss. The trail of his scent led me to a tent right by a large tree, one I was certain belonged to Dom. Sure enough, the black cat sat inside Dom's tent on a bed roll like it was put there just for him.

"Switching teams on me?" I admonished, bending so I could see into the tent. The cat just blinked at me in response.

"I'm definitely on the same team," someone said behind me. I whirled, Artemis out before I could blink, and saw Dom with his hands in front of him in a '*don't shoot*' gesture. Confident he wasn't a shark about to bite me, I put Artemis back into her holster and Dom lowered his hands. "Sorry, didn't mean to give you a fright." I had to admit, with the smile on his face and his delish Australian accent, I was feeling this vampire. And maybe I wanted him to feel me too. Sue me.

"No harm. I'm just here for my cat." I reached behind me, pointing to him on the bedroll.

"Ahh," Dom said as he walked over to us. "I was wondering where the little mate came from." The vampire was standing very close, and I found it difficult to get enough air. It had been so long since I'd smelled a scent like his that set my blood on fire. He was so tall and there was only hard muscle underneath his shirt. I felt dainty beside him, a feeling I was very unused to.

Shaking my head to clear the cobwebs, I bent inside the tent, making sure I wasn't presenting Dom with my rear end, and retrieved Puss from his perch by the scruff of his neck. I brought one hand up to cradle his legs and straightened up again. He growled at me.

"Hey, kitty," Dom said in a cute baby voice. I'll admit, it was interesting hearing him say my name like that, and the responding heat all over had me flushed. "I meant him," Dom clarified with a grin as he reached to pet the cat. "What's his name?"

Shrugging, I adjusted the cat in my hands when he growled again and tried to hide my flushed cheeks by looking down at the fur ball. "I don't know. I just call him Puss."

Dom laughed, his cheeks turning a ruddy pink. "You can't

name a cat Puss! He needs a proper name. Names give things a purpose."

Oh god, he was a hippie.

I shrugged again and got another growl from the cat. "I dunno. He follows me around all the time. That's not really a purpose."

"Like your shadow?"

He was definitely that. I looked down at him and pet his fluffy face with my thumb. "I guess I can call him Shadow."

Dom smiled again and wiggled his finger on Shadow's forehead. He was so close, I could see the vein in his neck thumping along with his pulse. *I was so thirsty.* "Glad I can bring you around to my way of thinking."

I twisted, taking Shadow away from Dom's finger and removing the temptation to sink my fangs into the attractive vampire's neck. "Is that what that was? Hmm. Didn't seem like it. C'mon, Puss." I walked away, swinging my hips as I went.

SLEEP WAS hard to come by in my tent. Maybe it was being around so many people after so long. Maybe it was that I'd finally found my mom. Maybe it was that I'd spent most of my nights doped up on Night Shadow and I didn't know how to sleep on my own anymore. I should've felt comfortable having Arthur's familiar scent nearby, but all it did was agitate me. And as I lay there petting Shadow's soft fur, I tried to figure out exactly why I was upset.

Maybe it was because I'd tried to find my family for so long and they'd been right under my nose? Or the fact that Jason was still missing. I could've gone the rest of my existence without finding my parents as long as I found my little brother and took care of him. Maternal instincts were completely foreign to me, except when it came to Jason.

Shadow's yellow eyes disappeared when he blinked, and then reappeared like little globes of light. My fingers scratched under his chin and he immediately rolled over to attack my hand with his little teeth and claws. I let him, it wasn't as if he could pierce my skin. Vampires made good scratching posts, it seemed. He kicked at me and gnawed on my thumb until he shook his head and looked up at me as if peering into my soul.

Surrounded by the warmth of Shadow's little body, I somehow drifted off to sleep. I dreamed of a house. Dreams were so infrequent to me, I hardly knew the difference between a dream and a hallucination. This felt lighter, like a fairytale.

The house was old, almost ancient. A deep scent of rot and mildew drifted into my nose and I wrinkled it in disgust. The room I stood in had scattered debris on the aged, wooden floor. A doll. Scraps of lace. An old hammer. Something called to me, and in my dream induced trance I left the room and walked down a hallway with the same wooden floor. The walls bowed and shook with the wind, almost as if one strong burst would bring them crashing down. Finally, I reached the front door and my hand automatically went for the rusted handle, but a noise brought my attention elsewhere.

To my right was a room with broken chairs, the remnants of a dining table where a family once ate their meals. It turned into a kitchen, one I could tell had not been used to cook a meal for at least a few hundred years, judging by the antique stove and the lack of running water.

The noise came again, a rustling like shoes against paper. I left the kitchen to see a small pantry room with a boy sitting in the corner. His shoulders slumped in a way that saddened me, and I was drawn to him like a moth to a flame.

He had long, brown hair, dirty and tangled like he hadn't taken care of it in months. As I came closer, I saw the brown was simply a thick layer of dirt, and the hair underneath was black. In the boy's hand was a piece of paper and his skin was brown against ragged fingernails.

Another sound came, this time soft sobs coming from the boy's throat. I approached as closely as I dared and twisted my neck to see what was on the paper he had.

It was an aging photograph of my family.

Jason.

I burst awake, Artemis out and my breath coming in ragged gasps, the barrel pointed right at Arthur who crouched right outside my tent.

"Kitty?" he asked in his rough voice.

My body trembled all over and my hand shook so much

that I dropped Artemis onto the ground. Had my dream been real? My mom had had a dream long ago about her future life. Now that I recalled, she'd mentioned an old house. The same one I'd seen?

Was Jason.... Was he really wasting away like that? He'd seemed far too young for his actual age of thirty-five, the exact age I'd been when I last saw him. Maybe I'd seen the past, whatever happened to him after the sharks came. But he'd been so alone in that house. It was exactly what I'd feared would happen to him.

Gods, I was tripping.

Arthur was still crouched in front of me, his icy blues showing much more concern than I'd ever seen on his face. He didn't ask if I was okay, simply sat and waited for me to speak. I'd forgotten how much I liked him.

Pushing a strand of black hair behind my ear, I picked Artemis up and slid her back into her holster. "Sorry. I'll be up in a sec." He nodded and left without another word.

Shadow was missing again, but I packed up my stuff before leaving my tent and packing it up too. The group of Lycans and the two vampires were gathered around the fire pit, this time passing around some freshly scrambled eggs with fried potato wedges. Arthur handed me a plate, glancing at my bag snug on my shoulders with the clip fastened in front.

"Leaving?" Dom asked me as he walked up.

I met Arthur's stare and shook my shoulders to adjust the bag. "I've been looking for her for twenty years, Arthur. I'm not wasting another day here if she's nearby. Plus, you intimated she was in danger."

Arthur sat on one of the logs around the fire and patted next to him for me to join. I did and dug into my breakfast with the fork they gave me.

"We have to do this right," he urged. "One slip up and our plans will fail."

I put a mouthful of the lightly salted eggs to my lips and pointed my fork at him. "You have one day, or I'm going without you," I warned him, my mouth full of food. He nodded and we finished our breakfast in silence.

11

TEA AND PISTOLS

DREYA

*B*ang!

  The glass bottle on a fence in front of me shattered into a thousand pieces, mixing in with the sand on the ground. I pulled my pistol back and let a small grin come to my face. I'd gotten much better over the years.

Clara clapped her hands from her spot on the front porch where she and Lucas sipped tea from a dainty tea set, the likes of which I'd never seen anywhere in Salvation. We didn't have room for such luxuries.

"Fantastic, Dreya!" Clara shouted, cupping her hands over her mouth so I'd hear her better, even though she knew my hearing was perfect. Clara was delightfully human sometimes. She always treated me like she would any other person.

"Now she can shoot her ridiculous boyfriend," Lucas

added, miming shooting with his hand and blowing smoke off his fingertips.

"Darius isn't ridiculous, and you haven't even met him," I chided gently, and turned to shoot again, knocking an ancient soda can off the fence.

"Come have some tea, dear. Don't waste the ammo."

I clicked the safety off and walked to the porch where I laid the pistol on top of the porch railing. Clara poured me some tea and dropped in a precious drop of honey before she passed it to me. I held it in my hands, like a small baby bird kept warm with its mother's wings. A sip filled my mouth with the gentle but potent flavor of Clara's homemade rose tea. It wasn't my favorite thing to drink, but I loved being there with my grandparents, drinking tea, like nothing else mattered. Like the world still made sense.

I speak as if I knew what the world was like before, when I clearly didn't, but it was easy enough to imagine from all the stories people had told me. Somehow being at Lucas and Clara's house felt like a look into the past. They hadn't changed. They still made tea and baked bread, like nothing was different.

How I wished I could simply stay there with them and forget everything else, forget all the pain and danger, but maybe one day I'd grow tired of the simplicity, and that thought drove me back to Salvation after every visit to my grandparents' house.

"How are things?" Clara asked, as she always did. She

missed my mother deeply, and the look in her purple eyes almost made me feel saddened too.

I looked down at my tea cup, scratched at the side, taking another sip. "Mother is... fine. Dad tries hard to chase the shadows away."

Lucas scoffed slightly, his face half hidden by his tea cup. "Son-in-law better take care of her. I can still punish him like a schoolboy. You tell him I said." I nodded, trying not to smile. They didn't know I was keeping my visits a secret from my parents, ever since Thomas and I had discovered their home when we were young. Deep in his thoughts, Lucas's face fell, and he almost dropped his tea cup. "He can't chase the shadows away. The shadows are all she's made of now. If he chases the shadows away, there will be nothing underneath."

Clara put her cup down and quickly got up to come beside her husband so she could take his hand. She whispered some gentle, loving words before holding him to her breast and stroking his blonde hair.

The faraway look in his eyes, the expression on Clara's face as she soothed him, I knew he wasn't thinking of my mother anymore. His mind was on her, my grandmother, Anastasia. Just as I felt time was reversed at their home, Lucas was often stuck in the past. He'd be gone for hours, if not days, before Clara could bring him out of it.

My great-aunt/step-grandmother met my eyes with a sad smile. "You'd best be back. We'll be fine. Send your mother our love. Don't forget the package for her." She nodded to the small parcel on the table, and I took it before kissing her on the cheek. I'd tell Lisbeth the gift was from me so she wouldn't worry.

Leaving them behind once more, I stepped off their porch and followed the trail, past the covering of trees, and onto the dirt road that led to Salvation. Thomas stood waiting for me, a slain deer across his shoulders. He had a swipe of blood across his chin and he smiled at me like nothing was wrong. My heart sped up seeing his bright pink aura, but I tried to ignore it. I had to ignore it.

"Nice visit?" he asked me. He looked down at my hands to see the small, wrapped package. "Best put that in your pocket. Don't want them to see." He adjusted the deer and turned once I'd joined him on the road. I pressed the package into my jacket as we walked.

"Sometimes..." I started, and stopped, pressing my lips together to stop my words. I couldn't let go, not yet. I was so close.

"Sometimes what?" Thomas probed jokingly, moving his hip to the side to bump against mine. I remained silent, and when he realized I wasn't going to open up, he sighed and kicked at a rock in the road. "You're different, Dreya. I don't remember you being so tight lipped in high school."

My lips curled, and I 'humphed' low in my throat. "People change, Thomas. It's part of growing up."

"Maybe," he conceded. "But I don't think people change that much. Sometimes... I don't know. You'd get this gleam in your eyes, you reminded me so much of your mom. That's gone now."

Practiced patience.

Ahh, screw it.

"Maybe *you're* the one that's different, Thomas," I snapped suddenly, whirling on him. "Did you ever think about that?"

He burst out laughing at me, dropping the deer onto the ground with a thump. "*There.* That's her. With your icy blue eyes and your beautiful blonde hair. I almost forgot what the real you looked like."

I wanted to kiss him so much.

Instead, I clunked my foot onto the ground and stomped down the road without him. "You're such a *jerk*, Thomas!" I shouted over my shoulder. My enhanced ear caught the sound of him slinging the deer over his shoulders again and jogging to catch up with me.

"I might be a jerk," he conceded once we were back in step. "But at least I'm *me*."

I sighed and swiped some hairs that had fallen into my eyes. "You don't understand." The boundary gates of Salvation were in view and I couldn't keep talking with them looming over me.

"Don't understand what?" he asked as he stopped walking again. I continued down the path to the fence and Thomas grabbed at my jacket. "Dreya, what don't I understand?"

One of the Lycan guards approached us and nodded to me, silencing Thomas' protest. "Dreya, you're needed at home." My stomach fell. Gods, no. Not again. "Nothing bad," he explained when he saw my look of horror.

Thomas handed the deer off to one of the vampire guards and brushed himself off. "What's up, Martin?" he asked, addressing the Lycan.

Martin hesitated slightly, only for a second, but it was an eternity in my head. "Your mother has... visitors."

12

LOVE REKINDLED

KITTY

"**I** swear to all the gods, if you get us killed, I'm never forgiving you," I warned Arthur as the looming gates of Salvation came before us. Dom stood on my other side with Shadow on his heels, and he peered up to the city like it was a mystery. Several vampires and Lycans stood at the main gate holding guns, probably for the sharks if any came nearby.

"If I get us killed, your mother will turn my corpse into tiny little pieces," Arthur said. The bottom half of his face was covered with my mask, covering him enough that he might not be recognized. "I like my pieces where they are, thank you."

I smirked and wondered at him for a second. "Never thought I'd see you be snarky. My mom's sass looks good on you." I was greeted with a glare, but I still smiled back at him.

Having seen our approached, the guards were slowly coming towards us, checking for sharks as they went. They smelled us and immediately looked at Arthur in alarm. The mask was to fool the bleeders. Our kind wouldn't be tricked so easily.

"Arthur!" one of the vampires whispered as we got closer. Arthur nodded slowly, looking around for any humans within earshot. "What are you doing here? You're a wanted man."

One of the Lycans was less worried. "You here for her?" *Her.* They didn't even need to specify who they were talking about. Arthur nodded again in confirmation.

"We'd like it if you didn't tell the humans about..." I gestured to Arthur and squinted at the guards. How I wished I had mind control powers. The vampires and Lycans glanced at each other in wordless communication, but they didn't seem upset to see us.

The first vampire lowered his gun. "The humans don't have to know who all of you are." He looked over at me and lifted a finger, pointing at my head. "Put her goggles on, Arthur. Your eyes are memorable." I pulled my goggles off my neck and handed them to Arthur for him to put on over his blue eyes. He adjusted them and I couldn't help laughing.

"You look like Bucky Barnes."

I felt the glare from him even though his face was covering it.

"Shut up."

"Martin, Dreya should be back soon. Let her know the Countess has visitors," the first vampire said. The Lycan trotted off along the fence, disappearing behind a building. We followed the vampire to the gate and waited for it to be opened before it was locked behind us.

A prison. We were in a prison.

My skin crawled, my clothes seemed too tight, and I wanted to run in the other direction as fast as I could. Surely all the vampires and Lycans could hear my rapid pulse and ragged breathing. Dom's hand gently found mine and entwined my fingers with his. My skin came alive, almost distracting me from my anxiety. He didn't speak, just stayed that way beside me with my captured hand as the vampires cleared our visit with the bleeders. Shadow rubbed against my boots.

Next came the drug search. The vampires sniffed us all over —eww— and checked our bags for any stray Night Shadow. I'd wisely left mine with the Lycans. Then they shined a light in our eyes to check for dilation, and pronounced us clean. Shadow followed us out when we left the guard post with an assigned escort, a younger vampire.

"My name is David," the vampire said as we walked. He kept looking back at me, so much so that Arthur elbowed him. "Sorry. You just look so much like her."

Flicking my eyes to Arthur's masked face, I took my hand back from Dom and stuffed it into my jacket pocket, mourning the loss of contact instantly. "Like the Countess?" David nodded and slowed down so he could walk beside me. "Why do you call her that, if I may ask?"

David got a hazy look on his face as he smiled at me. "The

Countess brought us all here. She protects us, makes peace with the humans. She gave us a place to call home." Sounds exactly like her. Except Arthur's story tainted it all with a nasty shade of red.

"It's not true about her killing all those humans either," David continued, his face still hazy.

I found Arthur's face again, this time in horror. *What was he talking about?*

"I'm not quite familiar with this Countess," I said, trying to smile at David. Not like he'd believe that since we looked so much alike there was no question we were related. "Could you explain what you mean?"

David stopped on the city path we were on and stared at me in confusion, almost cracking a laugh until he saw how serious I was. "She's the Countess of Bathory. You know, the one from the stories. She supposedly killed all those people, hundreds of years ago. And now she's here, our matriarch."

Oh gods, the whole world has gone insane.

"She's not the—" Arthur cleared his throat to interrupt me, shaking his head where David couldn't see. Okay, interesting. Why were they keeping up this story with everyone? I played along. "I mean, wowwww!" I plastered my face with an impressed look and reached back for Dom's hand. I might've barely known him, but I needed the contact again. He took it without comment and held my hand tightly.

David led us forward, talking constantly about the city's history and all that they'd done as far as development and technology. We went into a market area and all the bleeder venders glared as we passed them. *Weird.*

Arthur looked out of place with his face covered, everyone staring at us like we were cancan dancers putting on a show at a Baptist church. The bleeders pointed and whispered to each other.

"...looks just like the Countess..."

"...can't believe they're letting in a drinker that dangerous looking..."

"...Governor Hendrix can't have let more of them in..."

Judgmental little a-holes.

David and Arthur got a few steps ahead of Dom and myself, so he felt safe to lean into my ear and whisper in a tone that sent a shiver down my spine, "I've never felt a hand quite like yours."

A scoff came out of my throat. "It's just a hand. It's not special." He *'hmm'd'* and straightened up. My legs were jelly from him being so close as he tugged me forward. I wanted to just stop and hear his accent in my ear again.

Focus, Kitty.

I shook my head and checked Shadow's presence at my feet. He trotted next to us like everything was fine. Eventually, David and Arthur stopped at a building in the center of town, a tall clock tower. There was a piece missing from the clock's face, large enough for someone to fit through and stand on the balcony overlooking the city. Vampire guards stood at the front doors, their nostrils flaring when we came into range, and they stared at Arthur in alarm but said nothing as David walked us inside.

Several scents hit me when I went into the building, and I caught two I knew very well. A single tear rolled down my cheek in relief. She was here. Dom squeezed my hand, and I remembered where I was again. David led us down the hallway and up several flights of stairs where the scents became stronger, a potency only associated with a living space.

"This is where the Countess lives," David explained to us.

Arthur sniffed, smelling no one else around except three people in one of the rooms. One of them I didn't recognize by smell, so it had to be my younger sister. "We've got it from here, David." The vampire nodded and left us on the floor to have some privacy.

I didn't wait for a verbal cue from the men beside me, I stepped across the carpeted hallway to the room I knew held my family. The door flew open under my hand and I saw them there at a kitchen table, like I'd always remembered them.

Knight with a stack of pancakes.

Lisbeth with another plate in her hands.

And a blonde-haired girl sitting between them.

That one tear was followed by many as a choked sound escaped my throat when I saw those purple eyes staring back at me. She dropped her plate in shock and it broke against the tiles, littering the floor with shards and pancakes. Knight got up so quickly, he knocked his chair over. The girl stood as well, and though I'd never seen her before, I knew she was the sister Arthur told me of. She looked nothing like me with her blonde hair, blue eyes, and tanned skin, but there was something in her face I recognized from my own.

"Kitty?" she asked in wonderment, the first of the three to find her voice.

Lisbeth ran, throwing her arms around me, and her body shook with sobs against my chest. I held her so close, so close that I wished I would never have reason to leave her embrace.

Finally. Finally, I was home.

She cried. I cried. The girl cried. I let Lisbeth go only to fall into Knight's arms and I held him just as tightly, with all the love I felt for him.

Dom and Arthur lingered in the hallway, waiting for us to finish our reunion. Or maybe unwilling to ruin mine with their own, but that changed when Lisbeth's body stiffened beside me. She'd caught a scent, one she recognized, and she realized who I'd brought with me. Arthur slowly came into view from the hallway, his face still covered. He walked inside the room and Dom closed the door behind them.

Arthur lowered the mask, pulling the goggles off as Lisbeth took one tentative step, then two towards him, her face dripping with fresh tears. If I was a vision of the past, Arthur was a ghost she thought she'd never see again. And it was then I knew that something had changed between them. When it had changed was unclear, but it was something that we'd all been waiting for, for so long it felt like their story was mine too.

As she finally reached her slow journey across to him, she confirmed my thoughts with a single action.

She stood up on her tiptoes and kissed him on the lips.

13

BROKEN PANCAKES

KITTY

I'd like to say that I looked away as my mother made out with the man she'd loved as long as I'd been alive, but I stood next to my half-sister and Knight, watching the couple like they were goldfish in a bowl, and as nauseating as it was, no one in the room could deny the raw, unfiltered love between the two. They kissed with a passion I'd only seen her have for Knight. The passion of real love.

With all that happening in front of me, I glanced at Knight just to see how he felt about it and saw him smiling with happiness at them. He looked down at me, putting a hand on my shoulder.

"Let's give them some privacy," he said in a whisper.

"I can hear you," Lisbeth murmured, pulling from Arthur's lips only for a moment. He gave her another tender kiss on the lips, on her nose, and her forehead, before holding her in his arms like she was a precious jewel. And even though he would've shot me for saying so, I could've sworn I saw tears on his face. "We were just..." Lisbeth tried before she broke out into a fit of tears. She buried her head in his shoulder and wrapped her arms around his neck to bring him closer.

"Having breakfast," Knight finished, like he'd been the one talking. "I'll clean this up and make more pancakes for everyone." He busied himself with the task as Dreya approached the hugging couple.

Arthur pulled away from Lisbeth only for a moment to bring Dreya into their embrace. "I haven't seen you since you were a tiny thing, Dreya," he exclaimed with his lips pressed to her hair. "I realize asking if you've been behaving is redundant considering who your mother is."

Lisbeth lightly smacked him on the arm and leaned in for another kiss. "I don't remember you being this mouthy before."

He ran a hand through her long curls and studied her face as if memorizing it. "Perhaps I became more like that which I missed, if only to ease the pain of absence." His hand settled on her cheek and she leaned into it like a cat with a contented smile. "Maybe I also picked up your eloquence," he admitted with, dare I say, a blush on his cheeks.

Dreya left their arms and held out her hand to me with a smile that didn't fit someone that came from Arthur. "I'm Dreya. Short for Alexandria. You're my sister Katherine, Kitty for short."

I took her hand and pumped it a few times. She had a firm grip, I respected that. "We are a family with nicknames."

"Except for Jason," she reminded with a grin. The mention of his name turned the room cold. I stiffened and dropped Dreya's hand as Lisbeth let Arthur go, turning to me with hope in her eyes. Hope I couldn't keep afloat.

"Have you seen Jason at all?" she asked me with a face that looked like it would break into pieces if I said no. I shook my head, looking down, because I couldn't bear to see her shatter. She sucked in a shaky breath of air, but she remained composed. Her bare feet patted on the tiles and she gave me a soft kiss on my forehead. "I've waited twenty years for my babies to come home," she breathed against my skin. I fell in her arms again and felt a small sliver of happiness flood into me. She sniffed and kissed me again before she stepped away to help Knight pick up the rest of the mess she'd made.

Dreya brought over chairs for us and we sat around the table as Knight and Lisbeth made more pancakes. Every few seconds, he leaned over and kissed her head as she wiped more tears from her cheeks. When they were finished, Lisbeth sat down with me on her right and Arthur on her left. She held both of our hands as we started eating, unwilling to let go in case we were a mirage that would fade if she looked away. Arthur kissed her hand before letting it go so he could eat, but even as I tucked into my stack of pancakes, Lisbeth kept my left hand in hers, leaving her plate untouched so she could stare at me.

"Mom," I murmured, wiggling my hand. "Aren't you hungry?"

She let out a nervous laugh and set my hand free, picking up her fork and cutting into her pancakes. "Dreya, what color am I?" I looked over at my half-sister and saw her squint, turning her head. What was she doing? People weren't colors. "Dreya can see auras," Lisbeth explained to the rest of us.

Dreya was still squinting when she took a bite of food. "You're cascading, like a rainbow waterfall. I hardly know where one emotion ends and another begins." She turned her blue gaze to me and looked me up and down. "You, on the other hand. Very red. Grey. And there right in the middle..." Her blue eyes got even smaller as she focused on whatever she was seeing. "Deep, encompassing blue." Her mouth tilted into a frown.

Ignoring her weirdness, I pushed a piece of the pancakes into my mouth and let out a noise that was not one I wanted to make around family. How long had it been since I'd had such a confection? Probably the amount of time between family visits. The sweet, savory maple syrup mixed with fresh blueberries and chewy pancake. Heaven.

Dom was very focused on my face when I met his gaze, and the expression he conveyed made me want to blush. I wasn't the type for such a feminine reaction, but I felt slightly red just the same.

Did I... like him? No way. We hardly knew each other. I'd known him for what, two days? This wasn't a sappy romance movie, for Christ's sake. A very back part of my brain started to wonder what his blood would taste like. Gods, Kitty! He's not a Salisbury steak! *Focus, focus.*

Dreya giggled at me, no doubt seeing some kind of color shift above my head with her powers. She glanced at Dom and back at me with a knowing look. Great. I'd known my half-sister for ten minutes and she was already teasing me. It was growing up with Jason all over again. Maybe worse since Jason didn't have vampiric powers. He would just turn into a wolf every time we had to do chores.

The thought of Jason had me back in that old house, looking at his filthy hair and tear-stained face. I shook my head several times to wipe the image away and took another bite of food.

"Dreya has to leave soon, so that gives us some time to catch up, Kitty," Lisbeth said with a smile. "I remember you dislike an audience when we're talking about personal things. Unless that's changed?" I met her eyes and shook my head, already feeling awkward about it. Talking with her again was probably one of the things I'd been looking forward to the most, but I also dreaded talking about my life for the past two decades without her.

"Off with your friends?" Arthur guessed, nodding towards his daughter. No doubt he felt as awkward as Lisbeth did, addressing the children they barely knew.

Dreya smiled anyway, looking as warm as melted butter. "I'm having tea with my boyfriend, Darius, and his father, Governor Hendrix."

A loud clang echoed through the room as Arthur dropped

his fork suddenly. "You're dating Darius Hendrix, David Hendrix's son? The human who runs this city, the one who banished me?"

There was a lot to unpack from that, but the main contender slipped from my mouth like poisoned slime. "You're dating a *human*?" I shrieked at Dreya, my food forgotten. My appetite disappeared faster than a candle at a Bath and Body Works sale. Dreya's dainty mouth opened and closed, and she set her fork down onto her plate, dropping her head.

"I forbid it," Arthur declared with a humph. Lisbeth whirled on him so fast, we all bent away from her in our chairs.

"*You forbid it?*" she ground out.

Knight sighed next to me and rubbed at his forehead. "Oh boy. Bro is back for less than an hour and he's already awakened the Kraken." He lifted my plate and handed it to me before picking up his own. "She might break the table. It's happened before." I raised my eyebrow at him and set my plate back down.

"I'm not a grenade, Knight," Lisbeth grumbled, her glare still fixed on Arthur. "We're talking later," she warned, and he nodded stoically.

The table was rather quiet for a few minutes until I broke the silence before re-thinking my words.

"You might not forbid it, but it's still *gross*. Dating a human is like dating a drink dispenser."

"*Kitty!*" Lisbeth screeched, slamming her hand on the table.

It broke.

Everyone's breakfast was on the floor, except for Knight and Dom who were holding their plates in the air. Dom took another bite as he studied the mess at our feet.

I yanked myself out of my chair and shoved it back into the counters with a bang. Since I'd already said too much, saying something else wouldn't hurt.

"I can't believe I looked for you for twenty years. I should've given up a long time ago."

And I left the room the way I came.

14

SISTERS

DREYA

We all sat around the aftermath of mother's fist hitting the table, several minutes after Kitty had left. Mother's eyes darted around the floor and her colors rippled all over the place, so much so that I had to look away. She stared at the mess, looking forlorn. Even though she was often gloomy, it had been a long time since I'd seen her that sad.

Standing up, she crumpled fists of her black dress into her hands. "Excuse me, I need to cry by myself." She raced from the table to her bedroom door, slamming it behind her.

Dom's lips smacked and he speared a bit of pancake, swirling it around a puddle of syrup before popping it into his mouth. "If this is what it's like in your family, I want to stay forever."

I stood and almost started pushing my chair in before I

realized I couldn't with the table broken. "I'm going to go talk to her."

Knight nodded to me, Arthur on the other hand asked, "Which one?"

"We've got this, sweetheart," Knight said with a smile, and he got up to start lifting the edges of the tablecloth to keep the shards of broken plate contained inside it.

I left the room and went down the hallway, following Kitty's scent up the stairway and out to the clock face. She stood outside, her arms on the bannister, looking out over Salvation like it held the answers to her deepest questions, her entire body bathed in deep, aching blue. It made me sad just looking at it.

"What do you want," she snapped without turning once she'd caught my scent. She tried to discreetly wipe her face off, but I still noticed as I stepped up beside her and put my arms on the bannister too.

Deep breath. Practiced patience.

"Want to know a secret?" I asked her, keeping my tone pleasant. She didn't move, so I took it as a good sign to keep talking. "Mother told me once she's never known how to get through to you."

"I'm sure she doesn't have that problem with you," Kitty clipped, kicking at the bannister.

"Of course she doesn't." That drew a snarl from Kitty, and I smiled back. "I'm nothing like her. Whereas you're almost her copy. Or rather, you're like grandmother, and we've both heard how they butted heads when they met."

"It's *awesome* getting advice from someone who barely knows me," she grumbled.

My patience slipped just enough for me to frown at her. "Fine. Be obstinate. I'm just trying to help you."

That made her pause and raise her eyebrows at me. "Your Arthur is showing." My smile sparked hers, and we laughed together, leaning on the bannister as we watched the city people walking on the streets below.

"Your comment about dating a drink dispenser isn't very fair, considering you drink vampire blood," I countered, bumping her shoulder teasingly.

"Touché, sister mine." She took a few strands of her long black curls and braided them absently. "I'm guessing a lot has changed with vampire society since I've been gone, if they're all okay with you dating a human." She stiffened just before I smelled Knight approaching the clock face and stepping through the hole to the balcony. We both turned to him and Kitty placed a hand on her hip, her mouth curled to the side. "Clearly I'm right, since you're fine with Lisbeth having a second lover. Or are you just hoping it'll be holding hands and chaste kisses from here on out?"

Knight's face almost twisted into a glare, but he settled on a stern dad look I knew well. "I didn't come up here for you to grump at me, Kitty." His head turned slightly in my direction. "Dreya, can we have a minute?" I nodded and left them on the balcony until I got to the stairwell. They were still in my line of sight, and if I pushed my senses out I could hear their conversation. Yes, I was eavesdropping. We'll add it to my list of sins.

"You're mad at your mother, which honestly is exactly what it was like before the drones came," Knight said while he approached the bannister and leaned against it next to Kitty. "I'm assuming you still hate me."

Kitty looked up at him and away, her fingers still working her hair. "No. I don't. That was just me being a child." Knight raised his eyebrows at her, clearly interested in finally hearing an explanation for her ire of him. "When I was young, I thought you were the reason Lisbeth and Balthazar weren't together. I got it into my head that one's parents should be together, and mine weren't."

"Let me guess, a boy told you that?"

She scowled at him, but her aura remained gloomy blue. "That's not the point," she asserted, almost confirming his words. "I never said my mentality was correct. I've since learned differently. And I'm sorry for how I used to treat you. It's been one of my biggest regrets in my travels."

Surrounded by a sudden burst of happy yellow, Knight leaned in to kiss Kitty on her curled head and they turned to take in the city again. "In regard to your mother and Arthur," Knight said after several minutes of silence. "I've been with her for a long time. If there's anything I've learned, it's that keeping her happy is the only thing I care about. She loves him, she's always loved him. And she loves me too. That's all I need to know. And for the record, I've always been okay with sharing her, it's just not something I discussed with you or Jason."

Kitty took in a breath and sighed it out. "I guess things really have changed."

Leaning his hip against the balcony, Knight ran a hand through his thick, black hair and smiled down at Kitty where she couldn't see. It was clear he loved her like he loved me, his two daughters by marriage.

"Our society and its rules are nothing like they were before. Those days are gone, and not just because we're living out in the open among humans now. But no matter how much has changed, there's still a place for you in our home. We've all been waiting for you and Jason to come back. You don't know how much we wished we could find you ourselves."

"Why didn't you?" Kitty asked him, and she turned her head enough where she saw me in the stairwell doorway. Quickly, I shut the door and planted myself against the wall, waiting for her to come after me and yell at me for eavesdropping. Minutes passed and the door remained closed, but I went down the stairs anyway, just in case.

I reached our floor and went down the hallway to my bedroom where I shut the door behind me. It was time to get ready for my tea date with Darius and his father, Governor Hendrix.

Sitting at my vanity dresser, I pulled one of the drawers open and got out my small and precious makeup bag. Makeup was a luxury that few could afford, even with the coupon books we were given. Mother and I had made our own items from beeswax and the like. It wasn't much, but it was something at least. I had tinted lip balm, mascara, blush, eyeshadow, and some eyeliner. Of course, as a vampire I didn't really *need* makeup to be pretty. It was the act of dolling myself up and feeling lovely that appealed to me.

Using sparingly low amounts of all my products, I admired my gently blushed cheeks, darkened eyes, and rouged lips. I looked very put together, just the thing for tea with Governor Hendrix. I changed into a stylish blue dress and pinned my two braids around my head like a rope.

Satisfied with my appearance, I picked up my small purse that had my tinted lip balm, my coupon book, and a few extra hair pins, and fit it across my chest. I left my room and heard a noise across the hall like someone had thrown a piece of furniture. I pushed my senses out to investigate and immediately regretted it.

It seemed my parents were making up for lost time. Loudly. And breaking things in the process.

The floor creaked in several places as I rushed down the hallway, my cheeks turning pink when I heard a picture falling from the wall in mother's bedroom. Down the stairs and to the second floor, I stopped at the door that led to the Hendrix apartment. Catching my breath, I pushed a few strands of my hair aside that had escaped my pins before pushing the door open.

Two human guards stood with guns right outside the stairwell, and I nodded to them before turning and continuing down to the Hendrix living room. The door was open when I stepped up to it. It was the same floor plan as our home, but the two rooms looked very different. While ours was warm and home-like, theirs was very organized and streamlined with no paintings, trinkets, or decorations to speak of.

"Dreya!" Darius exclaimed from the sink when he saw me. Pink surrounded him and it brought a smile to my face. He approached me and kissed me on the cheek. Governor Hendrix stood by the fridge, busy with something on the tray they were setting up. He turned and smiled at me with a nod. His colors always frustrated me. I'd rarely ever seen him any shade other than what I could call clear. No emotions at all. Ever. Not even when he looked at Darius.

To say it made me not trust him was an understatement.

"Governor Hendrix," I addressed respectfully.

"Hello, my dear," he responded with another nod, the warmth of his smile not reaching his eyes. "We're almost finished, if you'll have a seat on the sofa." I left them in the kitchen and walked the short distance to the blue couches, sitting on the edge of one.

Darius brought the tray and placed it on the coffee table, sitting next to me while his father sat across from us. Darius poured his father's cup first and handed it to him before pouring mine. It would've been just a normal day if I didn't feel so unbelievably uncomfortable.

"How have your studies been after high school, Dreya? Have you re-considered the offer to join our medical staff? You have an aptitude for it." The Governor sipped from his china cup and leaned back into the couch.

I took my tea cup and sniffed it before sipping, drinking in the musky scent of the black tea leaves. Somehow, I found myself wishing it was rose petal tea. Maybe because the company would be better.

Patience. Breathe.

"I'm still thinking it over," I answered, smiling at him and making sure it reached my eyes. "I have a lot of things to consider right now." Darius poured himself a cup and leaned back to drink it.

We sat awkwardly for a few moments, but it wasn't uncommon for tea time at the Hendrix home to be silent and awkward. After a prolonged silence, and a few refills on my part of the warm tea, Governor Hendrix continued speaking as if we'd never stopped.

"I believe you have a birthday coming up, Dreya. Would you like us to reserve the community hall for it? We have the working music system now, we could get some records out and make it an affair. What do you say?" He smiled warmly at me even though the bland colors swirling over his head were anything but happy yellow.

I set my tea cup down, no longer having the stomach for more. "I don't like birthdays very much. Vampires don't really celebrate them." While that was true, we'd since learned to appreciate the holiday living among humans, despite my mother's continued protests about it.

I was making feeble excuses, and the look on the Governor's face said he knew it.

"Oh, come now," the Governor insisted, his tea cup

joining mine on the tray. "I know we haven't known each other for very long, considering you've only been with Darius for a year now, but birthdays are a Hendrix tradition. We never let them go uncelebrated, right, Darius?" Beside me, Darius also put down his tea cup and put a comforting arm around my shoulders. I felt slightly happy at his touch, though it didn't soothe me.

"Dad, she doesn't want to celebrate," Darius defended.

Governor Hendrix's square jaw twitched slightly, and he gripped at his knees before letting them go. "Why ever not?" he asked, in his same warm tone that wasn't quite as gentle as before. I could've easily broken every bone in his body without breaking a sweat, but his demeanor still terrified me.

Darius rubbed at my arm when I tensed up. "Because her real father isn't here to celebrate with her."

My entire body froze, tensing up with enough anxiety to kill a horse. *When had I ever told him that?* Maybe I'd said something about missing him, that was true, but never in that context. The more important question was, *had Darius just ruined everything with his big stupid mouth?*

The Governor shifted his legs and I could tell he was struggling to keep his face straight. "Arthur is a criminal."

I placed my hand on Darius's knee so he'd keep quiet, *damn him.* "I'm aware, Governor. I'm afraid Darius might've misunderstood me. I do miss Arthur, and I do wish he could be here with me, but he broke the law." When the Governor's face slightly relaxed, I decided to take a chance, even though my entire body was screaming for me to leave immediately.

"You've turned Salvation into a thriving city where everyone gets a second chance. Perhaps I am naïve, but one of the things your son has taught me is that forgiveness is one of the best traits we can have in this life."

Laying it on thick, much?

I cleared my throat and looked down at my shoes, my face the picture of doe-eyed innocence. "I'm afraid I've spoken out of turn."

"Nonsense," Governor Hendrix assured, and I raised my eyes to him, displaying warm relief I didn't feel. "It's important for women to speak their mind." He said no more and stood up from the couch, prompting us to do the same. "Always a pleasure, Dreya. And remember to come by any time."

I left the room, feeling a chilling wind upon my back, and I shivered in fear.

15

THE WHITE ROOM

KITTY

*K*night and I stayed on the balcony for at least an hour, mostly silent as we surveyed the buildings in front of us. He seemed distracted by something, but eventually his face lit up like an oven timer had gone off and he kissed my head, turning to the clock.

"We can go downstairs now," he said with a smile.

I lifted a skeptical eyebrow at him. "Why couldn't we before?" As an answer, he avoided looking directly at me and studied the clock face like it was a television screen. "Oh *gross!* Seriously?"

He shrugged, but grinned all the same, and I wanted to smack him for making me picture Arthur and my mom doing it. "They've got a lot of time to make up for."

I leaned my backside against the railing and crossed my

arms over my leather jacket. "When did she, you know, realize?"

"Realize that Arthur's excuses were bullshit and she's been in love with him for fifty-five years?" He snorted. "It was after they banished him. She felt lost, like a puppy away from its mother. Crying all the time. Eventually she told me he'd admitted his feelings a long time ago and while she felt the same, he'd hurt her so badly she wasn't ready to accept him back. She was getting closer and closer to it when he was taken away, and not having him around made her realize just how much she still wanted and needed him. Her feelings for him had gone neglected for so long, just the thought of finally having him back in her arms after all this time had her shaking. After that, it was just a weight on her, having to live without half of herself. Or a third, I suppose," he added with a laugh. I was still skeptical, and he noticed as he glanced at me. "I know it's not a-typical vampire. But I'm fine with it. Arthur and I have had an understanding since the drones came. I couldn't continue seeing them longing for each other, it hurt too much. Not because she wanted another man, because I knew she wasn't complete without him. And maybe I wasn't either." Shaking his head like he didn't understand the words coming from his mouth, he nodded his head toward the broken part of the clock face and started walking across the balcony. "Come on, you need to talk to your mother."

I hesitated, frowning. "Is it... safe?"

He snorted again and paused to... listen? Smell? Ugh, *so gross.* "Yep. It's safe."

Groaning, I followed him inside the hole and across the insides of the clock to the stairwell. We went down a few flights until he stopped at a landing and opened the door for me, then we walked down to the room we'd been in before. Lisbeth stood at the sink, busy cleaning the dishes, with Arthur behind her, holding her in his arms and kissing her on her dark head. His chin fit perfectly on top of her head, and the scent coming from them was pure *gross* love. I looked away with an ache in my chest. Not because my mom was cuddling with someone, because it had been so long since I'd been cuddled like that.

"Man on the floor," Knight joked, rapping his knuckles on the doorframe. Lisbeth turned, despite Arthur still holding onto her. She shucked him off and folded herself into Knight's arms when he approached her. He sniffed at the left side of her neck where he'd bitten her decades ago to mark her as his mate. It was still pungent after all this time. "Smells like me." Then he sniffed the right side of her neck, of which now carried the scent of Arthur's bite. "Smells like icicle breath." Arthur flipped Knight off over Lisbeth's shoulder where she couldn't see. Knight stuck his tongue out at the vampire and leaned down to place a kiss where Arthur had marked Lisbeth's skin and drew her closer to him in a loving embrace, and surprisingly he didn't flinch when Arthur's arms came around to hold both of them to him.

I cleared my throat, not even budging them from their cuddles with the sound. "Where's Dom?" Arthur shrugged apathetically, per his usual demeanor. No amount of time with my mother would change that part of him.

Lisbeth let Knight go finally, kissing him deeply on the lips and planting her feet on the ground again. "You two go, Kitty and I need to talk." She turned and gave Arthur a long, mournful kiss, held her nose against his for a few moments as they breathed the same air, finally after so many years, and turned him towards the door with a light shove.

With the men gone and the door closed behind them, Lisbeth nervously ran her hands along her skirt a few times. "We've been apart for so long, I hardly know how to speak to you, Kitty," Lisbeth said, breaking the silence. "I am sorry if I said anything to upset you."

I shook my head. "No, I was... being a jerk." Something brushed against my legs and I looked down to see Shadow's yellow eyes staring back at me.

"Will you tell me what you've been through all these years?"

I met her expectant gaze and looked down again. "There..." I swallowed a lump in my throat. "There are some things that even I'm not ready to face, but... I'll tell you what I can."

She nodded, satisfied. "That will be enough." Bending at the waist, she picked Shadow up and scratched at his chin. "I can't remember the last time I saw a cat. He's a cute thing." Shadow started purring and rubbed his head against her chin.

Traitor.

She carried him to a couch in the other part of the room

and I sat in a wicker armchair across from it. "Where shall we start?" she opened, her fingers running along Shadow's fluffy back.

The memory of our last meeting at the airport ran through my head, and a slideshow of all the events afterwards had me falling down a well of despair until I felt as if I couldn't breathe.

"Kitty, it's alright," her voice came beside me. "Breathe. Focus on Shadow." My chest finally moved and I gasped in a breath, seeing a fuzzy image of Shadow on the couch licking at his forearm. He came into focus and I felt Lisbeth's hands on my shoulder. "That's it. Come back," she soothed. My cheeks were wet, a single tear rolling down one side of my face. She reached for a tissue box, grabbing me a few to wipe my face with. They were scratchy and beige, and she laughed when I stared down at them. "They're biodegradable. Everything here is." Satisfied I was okay for the moment, she sat on the coffee table in front of me and kept my hands in hers. "Don't think about the bad memories. Tell me about what happened when those were over."

Taking a ragged breath, I sniffed and tried to pick a spot in time that wasn't a black hole of pain. Not an easy thing to do considering I felt like that all the time.

"I started looking for you after about five years had passed. Before..." I gulped. "Before then, I tried to ask anyone we saw if they'd seen you, but we were so busy trying to help the humans in Canada. I went to our home in New York, but it was empty. All the scents were gone, there was nothing to track, so I just started walking. I fed off the sharks when I found them." She raised her eyebrows at me, probably having never heard the street terms our kind used outside of Salvation. "Drones," I clarified, and she nodded. "I walked for hundreds of miles, for what seemed like a lifetime. No matter where I went, there was never a familiar face. Blee... humans started treating me differently. They stopped trusting our kind. And I had to stop trusting them too." I chewed on my lip until I tasted copper. "Eventually I found a working solar cycle, and with the aid of a welcoming vampire coven, discovered I'd been wandering around in the desert for six years. So then I drove for another six years, from town to town, killing sharks and trying to get information from anyone who could still talk. Then one day someone said they'd seen a vampire with icy blue eyes buying Night Shadow." Lisbeth hitched in a breath and sat back, letting my hands go. I looked away from her, ashamed over what I was about to tell her. "I chased down every dealer I could find, going all over the Midwest. There were certain areas the humans told me to steer clear of, one of them being where this city is, though they never said it was a city. Just that the humans in this area weren't too kindly to drug addicts."

"*Kitty*," she swore under her breath with a reproachful look.

My defenses rose but I tried to stay calm, certain she would understand. "When I take Night Shadow, I can see the face of the vampire's blood it was made from. I figured if I ever saw yours, or anyone I knew, I could track down where it came from. Besides, don't be all judgy. I found your blood in one stash, so don't act innocent." Her mouth was pressed together in a thin line, keeping her silent. "I followed that one sighting of Arthur for the past three years, until it led me here. To you."

"I see." She got up from the coffee table and sat back down on the couch with the cat in her arms.

"Mom, how did your blood end up in Night Shadow?"

"This town has many secrets, Kitty," she deflected. "And eyes and ears everywhere." Her eyes darted to the door that led to the hallway and her hands never stopped petting Shadow's fur. The story Arthur had told me was slowly coming to light, and I was beginning to think that it was much worse than he'd guessed.

Knowing she wasn't going to talk further, I struggled with trying to find something we *could* talk about. "Jason," I said suddenly, and her eyes came to rest on my face. "What happened to him?"

"Hmm," she mused with a haunted sigh. "We sent him away with Balthazar to keep him safe. That was the last we saw of him." The question I'd asked Knight on the balcony came back to me.

Why hadn't they left Salvation to search for us?

He hadn't given me an answer, and I doubted she would either. I watched her pet Shadow with a hazed look on her face, and I realized her behavior reminded me of her father, the crazy Lucas.

Her face brightened quickly enough to startle me. "I bet

you're thirsty. Have you drunk today?" I shook my head, prompting her to stand. She brushed her hair back from her neck and waited for me to come closer to her.

She was offering me her blood? I hadn't drunk from her since I was an infant. It felt like being offered baby formula. Still, I hadn't had real vampire blood in so long. I stood, the wicker chair creaking underneath me with the effort, and I approached her, my fangs already dropping as the perfume of her blood called to me. When I was close enough to see the pulsing vein in her neck, she grabbed my arms and pulled me flush against her.

"Let me drink your blood, Kitty," she whispered so quietly I almost didn't hear. Even after twenty years apart, I trusted her, and I leaned my head to the side. Quickly, she dropped her fangs and latched them onto my neck, piercing the skin and causing a jab of momentary pain, making me wince. She was done in less than ten seconds, keeping me close to her when she'd finished, pressing our noses together.

"*There. That's better,*" she said inside my head.

"*What the... mom?*" I thought back to her.

"*Shut your eyes,*" she told me, and I did so.

Immediately, I was transported into a white room where we stood facing each other. We were both wearing white pantsuits, a look I'd never have on in real life.

"Pretty neat trick, right?" she said with a grin.

"*Are we in the Matrix?*" I asked her, turning this way and that to see every angle.

She giggled. "No. I'm inside your head. We can talk without worry in here. No one will hear us."

"*When did you learn how to do this?*" I shrieked out and flipped my hands around. "This is *so cool!*"

Her smile fell and she looked down at her sandals. "I'm afraid this particular skill was learned out of necessity." Suddenly there was a white couch for us to sit on. She sat and patted the spot next to her. "You need to hear the real story about the night Arthur was taken away."

16

SALVATION WITH A COST

KITTY

*P*ractically running, I sat on the couch next to her and watched her sigh a few times, shutting her eyes to steel herself for what she was about to say.

"We came to Salvation when Dreya was very small. I'm sure Arthur has told you this part. We thought it was a safe haven. Governor Hendrix took us in and promised us refuge from the drones in exchange for our service as protectors of the humans. Once more Lycans and vampires came, he quickly realized that they viewed me as their leader, even if I'd pissed off more than a few of them by going public to the humans. We had a good partnership for a time. And then..." she trailed off, fiddling with her fingers. "He started requiring us to all donate blood. Not the humans, just the vampires and Lycans. He said that the medical team was researching the healing properties of our blood, and no one thought it was strange until he asked for more, and more, insisting it was for medical purposes. I followed him to where he took the blood once it was donated, and I found a room where the humans were making Night Shadow. With our blood."

"*Damn it*," I swore, and it echoed across the white space.

She nodded, her eyes absent. "I confronted him, and I told him we refused to give him more blood. I threatened to take all the vampires and Lycans with me. And he..." The deep, choking sound she made echoed as well. "He burned Cameron and Merrick's home to the ground. With them inside."

I instantly got to my feet and let out a string of curse words I was certain the world outside my head could hear. Lisbeth was crying silently during my tirade and didn't stop me.

"After that," she continued once I'd quieted down, still pacing angrily. "He made it clear that Dreya would be next." I swore again, not bothering to hide it anymore. "I packed up as much as I could carry in our bags and I tried to get us out. When the guards found us, they blinded me with a flashlight and forced three pills of Night Shadow down my throat. Hendrix knew that Arthur or Knight would take the blame, and if I was separated from either of them, he'd have my Achilles' heel, because it would fuel any threat to taking the other away as well. And he was right."

I had to wipe my face on my large white sleeves so I could see clearly past all the tears.

"He banished Arthur to the wastelands, and he confined

me to this building. I haven't been outside in thirteen years. Any step out of line, Dreya or Knight would die. I knew it. He knew it. And I was stuck here in these rooms while my babies were out in the world, lost and alone, and I couldn't even tell my mate what was going on." More tears trickled down her cheeks, and she sobbed as she took a breath. "Hendrix created my persona of the Countess, drawing from my family background so more of us would come in. So more of our kind could become his prisoners."

I fell onto the couch and threw my arms around her, and we both cried together. I was certain that outside my head, both our faces were as wet as a faucet. Once we'd calmed down, she wiped at my face and sniffed a few times.

"Kitty, I'm pregnant."

"*Already?*" How long had it been since Arthur had returned? A few hours? She couldn't know yet, right?

She managed a small laugh. "No. It's Knight's baby. I haven't told him yet. I wasn't sure how to, knowing that it would only be another tool for Hendrix to use against me." Her warm hands took my cold ones. "I need you to take Dreya away from here and find Jason. I won't bring another child into this world with my life at stake, and I won't risk rebellion with my children in the line of fire. Take her with you, and her friend Thomas. He'll protect her."

"We have no idea where Jason is at. He could be in a different country. It could take us years to find him." The old farm house came to me and I gripped her fingers. "I had a

141

dream about him. He was at an old house, holding a picture of us."

She turned her head in thought. "Was it a white house? With a broken dining table to the left of the door?"

My head twisted in surprise. "How did you know that?"

Her smile of relief lit up her face. "I know where he is." A noise in the real world interrupted us. Lisbeth looked around the white space and back at me. "It's Knight and Arthur." Though my mind was engaged in the scene she'd created, my body felt her hand leave my side in the physical world, and the two men joined our circle.

They popped up beside us on the couch.

"What in the living hell is this?" Arthur exclaimed, taking it all in.

"Freak mind powers, baby," Knight answered, leaning back on the couch with his hands behind his head. Clearly, he'd been here before. "My girl can do it all. Or, our girl, I should say."

Lisbeth gave me a quick smile and then she related everything she'd told me about Hendrix and the real face of Salvation. It was worth noting that she'd left out her being pregnant. I suspected the thought of rebellion would turn both men against her plans if they knew she was expecting.

Knight's first reaction was to stand and pace the perfectly white floor of the area. "You..." he started and stopped. "You kept this from me, this whole time. For thirteen years." His knuckles popped as he made fists and let them go. I felt a shimmer of his inner wolf come out, here in our minds where it didn't require the moon to show itself.

"If you'd have known, you would've freaked out," Arthur noted evenly, as if he hadn't just been dropped the same bombshell.

"You're damn right I would've freaked out," Knight ground out, shaking his finger at the other man.

Lisbeth had tears in her eyes again and she gave Knight a look that asked, begged, for understanding. "I couldn't risk Dreya. You had to be in the dark."

Puffs of hot breath came from Knight as he continued pacing, his fingers running through his hair so much that I thought he might pull it all out. The sound of his feet on the empty floor was deafening.

"I'm not mad at you, love," he said finally. "I'm mad at myself that I didn't see. You were holding this inside for so long and I didn't see. I mean, I suspected something was wrong when you stopped leaving the clock tower and started using your mind palace for every single conversation between us. But this... it's so much worse than anything I'd imagined." His feet went still, and he stopped next to me. "What now? How are we getting free?"

"Kitty and Dreya are leaving to look for Jason. Kitty had a vision about him, he's at your family homestead in Texas." Ohh. That's what the old house was. "While they're gone, we will do what we must to get away from Hendrix."

"I'M NOT LEAVING," Dreya declared once we'd brought her into the family meeting, in the real world this time. Lisbeth had been paranoid enough to bring us into her mind palace, but now that we knew the basics, she felt safe speaking out loud. Plus, we were already harboring a fugitive, so talking about this Hendrix dude wouldn't get us in more trouble. "Darius won't let his father hurt me, and I can do more at his side than I can outside of Salvation."

"Somewhat unconvinced," Arthur muttered, and Lisbeth lightly smacked at his arm to hush him.

"You'd be putting your life at risk, regardless of Darius's involvement," Lisbeth warned her, her purple eyes as serious as I'd ever seen them.

"I'm confident," Dreya assured with a nod. "Trust me."

And with an answering nod from Lisbeth, we were all in agreement.

17

SAFE TRAVELS

KITTY

om and I left Salvation behind after several tearful goodbyes that I was trying to push from my mind. Shadow followed us out of the city and we continued down the road as the gates were locked behind us.

I'd been instructed to loop Dom in as soon as we couldn't be overheard, and did so once the city was a blip on the skyline. He stopped, turned, and squinted at the horizon. Just barely, we could see the tallest buildings standing ominous and proud.

"They may not be there when we get back," he said absently, more to himself than me.

I tilted my chin and stared at the distant city with a venomous sneer. "If they're gone, I'll raze that city to the ground like Godzilla. With a smile on my face."

When I looked back at Dom, he was appraising me with a

surprised, and dare I say impressed, look. "Arthur said your mom was intense. I guess you are too."

I humphed and turned back around, my shoes crunching on the dirt as I continued walking. "Spent a lot of time with that one? He's not much of a sharer. How much do you even know about him, I wonder?"

Dom shrugged his shoulders underneath his large camo back pack. "Arthur is a complex person."

"Is that polite speech for weirdo?"

He snorted at me and picked up a pebble to toss off a towering rock formation next to the road. "He's kind of your dad now, isn't he?"

The image of my mom doing it was back, *so gross.*

"Bleh, gag, don't remind me. I have three dads now. That sounds like a very bad sitcom." I had plenty of time to get used to it. Assuming they were all still... alive... after all this was over.

By nightfall, we made it back to the Lycan camp where I'd left my motorcycle. Simon took the news about Arthur and Salvation in strides, and he promised to keep his eye out for anyone coming from the city. I spent a restless night in my tent with Shadow curled against my back. It felt like I'd just closed my eyes when Dom shook at my tent to wake me up. I didn't put Artemis in his face, so he got off lucky.

We packed up some jerky from Simon before saying good-bye, and with Shadow zipped up into my jacket and Dom sitting behind me on my cycle, we sped off across the dusty road.

ACCORDING TO KNIGHT, his old homestead was somewhere in the mid-west part of Texas. He couldn't give an exact area because he hadn't been there since roads were invented, but we were certain that if Jason was still there, he'd have marked his territory pretty well. From bleeder chatter I'd heard, Texas was swimming with sharks. No bleeders to speak of. It was why I'd never searched there before now, and I felt like a stupid ass for leaving out the one place where Jason might be. He was a pack animal by nature, so if there weren't other Lycans or bleeders around, why would he be way out in the middle of nowhere?

Questions we would discover. Hopefully.

As Lisbeth hadn't actually let me drink from her, I was beginning to feel the ache of hunger from going several days between feedings, not to mention the bullet holes that had finally healed, taking more of my blood for the effort. I needed blood soon or this trip would go sideways fast. Dom was still clutching at my middle on the motorcycle, unaware how hungry I was, and that he was probably on the menu if I got too starved. Drink dispenser, indeed.

I pushed the hunger away and tried to focus on something good. Something worth celebrating. I'd found my family, and I was on my way to find Jason. Finally. Thalia had been right. Pushing on and never giving up had paid off.

My eyes closed for a split second and I remembered the way she used to smile at me. I missed her so much. Even after all the years of her being gone, I'd never actually spoken aloud a single word about her. Maybe I never would.

"Eyes on the road, kitty cat," Dom snarked in my ear as he slapped his hand on my shoulder to wake me up. My eyes popped open and we were swerving off the road, easily corrected with a twist of the handlebars. "Thinking about my dashing good looks?"

The words came easily, despite my mood. "Better. About a gorgeous woman."

"Oh, that is better! Do tell."

I shook my head and pushed my foot onto the throttle, picking up speed down the road. We covered a lot of ground before the sun set and the bike engine stopped working for the night. We got off and I rolled the bike down the highway with Dom on the other side. Shadow wiggled around in my jacket until I let him out so he could follow us.

"Hope we find humans tomorrow. I'm mighty thirsty. How about you?" He raised his eyebrows at me with a smile.

"I'm fine," I lied. No need to worry my food supply. I imagined all the ways my mom would scold me if she heard me talking like that. The night air quickly turned colder, but we kept walking until we found an abandoned motel. With no sharks within sniffing distance, Dom used a jimmy he had in his backpack to open the glass motel doors. Once we were both inside, we closed them again and they stayed put with a whoosh.

The lobby of the motel was covered with a thick layer of dust that puffed out with every step we took. We went past the breakfast buffet area and down towards the rooms. Several doors were open, letting in all the dust, but we found one that was sealed tight. Dom used the jimmy again and got us inside before I shut the door, locked it, and put up the chain locks. No sharks could get inside now.

Dom leaned his backside against the sink that waited right outside the door, looking me over slowly in a way that heated my cheeks. "Too bad there's no running water here. I could use a bath. Maybe we could share?" Ignoring him, I turned and walked over to the large king-sized bed and dumped my bag on it. "Sorry if I'm bothering you," Dom apologized, coming into the bigger part of the room.

I paused and looked up at him, seeing his face had turned very serious, a look I could tell he wasn't used to. "I'm not used to... flirting. Or people for that matter. I've been on my own for a long time." Shadow jumped up onto the bed and I scratched his head while unpacking a few things from my bag before removing my jacket.

"Arthur was the same way. Did you know that he once went several decades without speaking? It's why his voice sounds scratchy all the time."

Straightening, I clutched my toiletries in my arms and walked past Dom to the sink. "I probably know more about Arthur than you do." I set my stuff down and opened my container of wipes. I kept them fresh and moist with water, perfect to help get me clean without a shower. Taking several, I handed a few to Dom before I went to town on my dirty face. "How old are you?" I asked him as we cleaned ourselves.

"About as old as you, I suspect. I was born before the event. I remember movie theaters. Theme parks. High school." He shuddered and took more wipes, running them over his light blonde stubble. "Ugh, high school. One thing I'm glad we don't have to suffer through anymore."

I swiped at my temple and turned slightly to look at him. "I was home schooled. You went to school with humans?"

He raised his blonde eyebrows with a grin, and gods above if my heart didn't skip a beat. "You didn't? Oh, now I really feel like a freak."

"You should," I smarted, looking back at the mirror with a smile. He threw a crumpled wipe at me as punishment and I dodged, not even stopping my path down my neck. The scoop neck of my gray shirt let me wipe all around my collarbone and I looked up to see Dom staring at my hands intently.

"Do, please, continue," he offered, smirking per his usual. I tossed the wipe at him, expertly hitting him square in the face even though he tried to move out of the line of fire. We both took more wipes for our arms, and Dom went back to the rest of the room while I removed my boots to attempt cleaning my feet.

"If only we'd stayed in Salvation long enough to bathe," I grumbled as several rocks fell from between my toes.

"Remind me to complain about your mom's sense of urgency." I rolled my eyes and heard Dom picking something up before flopping onto the bed. Stepping back, I saw him, remote in hand, pretending to flip stations on the ancient, dead television. "Ugh, Golden Girls is never on when I want it to be."

My eyebrow quirked up at him. "You watch Golden Girls?"

His mouth contorted as he tried to look innocent. "Don't tell Arthur."

Snorting a laugh, I finished cleaning myself and crossed in front of the dead television to sit in an armchair next to the bed. I lifted my still kind of gross feet onto the dining table and folded my hands on my stomach. It grumbled loudly in protest of my neglect.

Dom looked around like the tummy rumbling was coming from the walls. "I hear dead people. They're telling me... eat some jerky."

"Mmm," I groaned and shut my eyes, trying to ignore the pain in my throat. I was *so* thirsty. When was the last time I'd fed? The fact that I had to ask was bad. "If only that's what it needed." Dom went still, like a human trying to be immobile so the Tyrannosaurus doesn't notice them. I peeked one eye at him, heard his heartbeat speeding up, and closed my lid again. "Better watch out. You're looking mighty tasty right about now."

"I've never been fed from before," he admitted, his voice sounding oddly curious. "Could you control me if you wanted?"

I fanned my hands out in a shrug, ignoring the huskiness in his voice and how warm it was making me. "I've only fed from people older than me or too close to my age. I suspect

I'll be able to eventually, but ethics would prevent me from becoming the evil warlord of my dreams. Though I'd definitely wear an awesome outfit either way. Something with a cape."

"Maybe one of those evil up-turned collars too, while you're at it," Dom joked back. "I could be your evil henchman."

My stomach bounced under my hands as I laughed and opened my eyes to see his two-toned gaze on me, his back against the bed's headboard. Something about it made my stomach flutter, and I stood up to rid myself of the sensation.

"We need to find sharks and bleeders tomorrow," I informed him while grabbing my bag from the bed to lay on the floor. I climbed up the bed's ancient comforter and plopped my head on one of the pillows next to where Dom sat. It smelled like dust, but it wasn't covered in it at least. "If we don't feed, we'll never get the chance to find Jason."

"I'd never let you go hungry," Dom assured me from above my head. My mouth opened as I tried to respond, but I'd already started drifting off to sleep.

18

FULL BELLIES

KITTY

The next morning, I found myself waking up with a warm body behind me, snuggled into my backside, curved perfectly to fit against me. I started wiggling into it, feeling all the planes and bumps, before I realized who was lying behind me.

"*Bloody hell*," I shrieked and rolled off of the bed, landing hard on my butt on the floor. "*Gods above*," I shrieked again, my hands reaching to where Artemis lay and I picked her up to point at Dom still on the bed, Shadow lying at his feet.

He held his hands up and his pulse thundered on his neck. He smelled *so good*. "Kitty, calm down, I wasn't..." A curse word escaped his lips, and he started struggling to get free from the white cotton sheet we'd been sleeping under. "Kitty, calm down," he repeated, his hands still out to protect himself as he walked around the bed.

Sweet, crimson, flowing blood. So long... so long since I'd had anything except stinking shark blood. I was *so hungry*.

Taking advantage of my state, Dom grabbed Artemis and tossed her on the bed, narrowly missing Shadow, before taking my hands in his. "You're going into a frenzy. How long has it been since you fed?"

My fangs were starting to drop, and I knew my eyes were glowing red with the tendrils of a frenzy coming over me. "I don't..." I swallowed, feeling the burn of thirst along my throat. "I can't even remember."

Dom swore again and bent to the floor, gathering up our things while I stood by the bed, my hunger right on the precipice of insanity, but somehow keeping myself from going over.

"So... thirsty..." I muttered when he took my hands again. Numbly, I followed him out of the room, down the hallway, out the lobby, and to my cycle with Shadow close behind us. Dom zipped Shadow into his jacket and mounted the bike with my hand still in his, and he tugged it to bring me onto the seat behind him. He thrust on the pedal to start the bike and raced out of the parking lot like we were on fire.

I felt like Frodo, gasping for air as he got closer and closer to Mordor, except I needed to drink vampire blood instead of destroying a golden bauble. Dom was my Sam, carrying me to Mount Doom, AKA. my next meal.

Run faster, Sam. I'm horribly peckish.

Dom used his senses to pinpoint the closest den of sharks, but it was still an eternity until we found them. I was a second away from fanging Dom in the neck when I caught their scent. Sweet, crisp sharks. Their blood just waiting for me, like a microwaved hot pocket. Dom stopped the motorcycle as we pulled into an abandoned city, not unlike the one where I'd left the drug dealers to rot in the heat.

The sharks were gathered in the middle of town, around what was once the city courthouse, a tall stone structure, untested by time for now. It was my beacon of hope, not to mention a full belly. Sizing up the large group of drones, I dismounted the bike and slowly walked across the old paved road, my every step causing them to take notice of me. Once I was far enough away from Dom, I flipped my hands out to form claws, my fangs dropped, and I screeched out a cry.

I charged.

The sharks ran to me, I met them with my claws out, and I hacked at the first two, grabbing one to my mouth to take a long pull.

Gross. But so good.

I tossed that one away and went to the next wave. They met the end of my claws as I whished by and flipped through them. Those that didn't end up as my food ended up in pieces. Once my belly was full and my hunger as sated as it could be on shark blood, I continued laying waste to them until none were left and I stood in a bloodied heap right at the center of their corpses.

Turning, I looked back at Dom on the bike, Shadow's head peeking out of his jacket. He stared at me with equal parts fear and fascination. Good. He should fear me. That'll teach him to snuggle me in my sleep. Turning the engine back on, he rolled the bike up and got off to approach me, side stepping the bodies around my feet.

"That was pretty wicked," he appraised, his mouth doing that quirky smile that made my stomach jump like a grasshopper.

I shrugged and some drips of blood fell from my fingers. "Wicked is good."

A gun shot came from above and the bullet hit the ground right next to Dom's boot, ricocheting off the concrete.

"Put your hands up, drinkers!" a voice crackled over an outdoor speaker system. I pinpointed the sound coming from the top floor of a faded red building next door to the courthouse. We faced it and put our hands up as instructed when a group of bleeders emerged from the front door, guns out and pointed at us. "Surrender your weapons," the voice said.

"You realize I can kill all of you without my gun, right?" I informed the bleeders when they approached. The biggest one broke from the line and put his hand out, wiggling his fingers for me to hand over Artemis. I did, throwing a pouty glare to the window where the speaker sat. Still pointing their guns at us, the bleeders led us inside.

It seemed I was destined to only see the inside of bars on my travels, because that's exactly what the place had been, or still was judging by the red-haired woman standing behind the wooden bar. She was doing the typical bartender thing of wiping at glasses with a towel that she threw over her shoulder when we approached, because bartenders never did anything else.

"You're a mess," she observed, her mouth curving up from the sight of me. I grinned back and licked at the blood on my hand while maintaining eye contact with her. She gave me a look that made my spine shiver. "Take a seat."

I grabbed one of the red barstools and sat on it while the bartender poured us something to drink. I downed it in one gulp, whiskey by the taste of it, and slammed the glass on the counter hard enough to echo but not hard enough to break it. Dom also drank his, without being dramatic about it.

"Thank you for taking care of the sharks," the woman said, downing her own drink. "It's been hard to leave this building since they showed up a few days ago."

"Guns don't work?" Dom guessed, throwing his head back to where the other bleeders stood with their rifles.

The bartender almost looked sheepish, and she poured herself another drink, tossing it back swiftly. "We ran out of ammo months ago."

I flipped my arm behind my head, wiggling my fingers at the bleeder who had done the same to me. "I'll take my gun, thank you." He pressed it into my hand and I slid her back into my holster.

"You from Salvation?" the woman guessed, her blue eyes looking us over. "I haven't seen drinkers in these parts for a time, to be sure. They're all at that city now."

"Speaking of which," I transitioned with a smile. "My friend here needs blood."

That made her pause, and her eyes darted back to the other bleeders, no doubt wishing they still had ammo. "We're not a blood drive, girl. We don't feed your kind."

Dom pulled his backpack to the side, unzipped a pocket, and pulled out a baggie of Night Shadow, which he tossed onto the counter. "Trade. Blood for Night Shadow."

Her eyes widened at the sight of the dark red-purple pills and she scratched at her neck in thought. I might've been immune to the addictive effects of the drug, but bleeders, vampires, and Lycans were not. Bleeders were especially susceptible to its charms, though they were at a very high risk for overdosing if they weren't careful.

"One bag for now, another tomorrow for more blood," Dom negotiated, his fingers drumming on the wooden counter.

The woman tried to look nonchalant as she leaned back against the shelves that held bottles and bottles of brown liquid. "As I said, we're not a blood bank." Her words didn't sound as convincing as before, making Dom expertly straighten up, his hand reaching for the baggies in a power move.

"Alright, we'll be on our way again," he said evenly. When his fingers closed around the baggies, all the bleeders seemed to close in on us, the bartender included, hoping to stop us from taking the drug away.

"Fine," the woman said with a sniff. "Two feedings, and that's it. You ask for more, or take what's not offered, I won't need ammo to end you."

Though she meant what she said, I held back a scoffing laugh because none of them could take us, but we had to go by their rules, and that meant playing along. Dom and I nodded, and one bleeder came forward with a curl of the bartender's finger. Dom slid off his stool and was onto the guy's neck in a flash, the room filling with the smell of copper blood. The bleeder shoved Dom away when he was finished and had a look of disgust on his face as he said some very unkind things under his breath about us.

The woman cleared her throat, her fingers closing around the baggie of drugs before we could stop her. "We have running water if you'd like to clean up."

Heaven.

WET KISSES

KITTY

By '*running water*' the bleeders meant a communal shower area at a public pool nearby. They'd connected the showers to well water so they magically still worked. I didn't care what format a shower came in, even with my perfect memory it felt like I couldn't remember the last time I'd had a bath.

The bleeders left us alone in the pool building since they didn't like being near us, and they were probably all going to get high off Night Shadow anyway, so we'd be alone for the night.

Dom and I walked past an empty pool area to the showers. The room smelled like rusty pipes and old shoes, but I didn't care. I didn't even care that Dom was standing next to me, I stripped down to my underthings and ran to the nearest shower head. It squeaked when I turned the handle, but sure enough, lukewarm water started coming out of the shower head and poured onto me like a holy baptism.

I let out a noise that probably wasn't wise to be making when I was so undressed. Dom didn't comment, he merely also got down to his skivvies and came to the shower beside me, letting out his own noise of contentment when the water hit his head.

The water rushed down my toes and turned the floor a crimson color from all the blood on my skin. I found a bar of soap on a ledge above my head and used it to scrub off all the red from every patch of skin I could reach. My bralette looked a little pink now, but I'd soak it after this to get it white again.

Dom held his hand out for the soap and I gave it to him, thinking he'd use it on himself. Instead, he lifted a finger and twirled it, meaning he wanted me to turn around. I did, pulling my long black curls to my front, and then his warm hands were on my back.

How long had it been since I'd felt someone's touch on my back like that?

Gently, he used the soap to get all the spots of blood where I couldn't reach, his hands moving over my flesh long after he'd finished scrubbing. He tugged on my arm slightly to pull me back under the shower head and rinse me off. I started moving away, but he grabbed at me again and I heard him rustle into his bag for something before he squirted a liquid onto his hand. His hands came back, but this time they were on my head, running through my curls with the shampoo he'd brought to get my hair clean.

"I had shampoo too, you know," I said in a half complaint. My body had started shivering even though the water was still pleasantly warm.

Dom laughed slightly and continued massaging the suds into my curls, the gentle caress of his fingers relaxing every muscle in my body. "Mine is better. Your mom gave it to me, it's for curly hair. She wanted to make sure your hair was cared for."

I dropped my eyes and smiled where he couldn't see. Even cornered and threatened, she was still looking out for me, with something as simple and insignificant as shampoo. Another tug from Dom's large hands and he helped me rinse all the shampoo out.

"Thank you," I said without meeting his eyes, mostly because I wasn't sure what I'd see on his face if I did. "Let me get your back too." He turned his back to me, handing me the soap over his shoulder, and I came up behind him, bringing the sudsy bar to his perfectly toned back. Suddenly I wasn't shivering anymore, I was as warm as a sunburn. Ignoring that, I ran the soap across all his plains and valleys, rubbing it in with my fingertips. "I never thought I'd get to shower again."

He laughed, the chuckle shaking my hand on his back. "Me either. Feels like it did before, when the world wasn't like this. Funny how something as simple as a shower can pull you back in time."

I was also floating back in time, but not to the days before the sharks came. With my fingers dancing across Dom's skin, I was back to the last time I'd had a shower, when Thalia was still alive. We'd stood under the spraying water, less dressed than I was with Dom, and it was decidedly more romantic in nature. Something about the memory was making me sadder than I'd felt in a long time. I'd tried to move on, I really had.

Maybe I was feeling vulnerable, maybe something inside me was trusting Dom more than I'd trusted anyone in so long. Trembling all over, I stepped closer to him and put my arms around him from behind, my hands clutching the skin right above his belly button. I held him to me under the warm water and I felt the patched-up pieces of my heart fall into a cluttered heap again.

Dom's hand came up and laid over mine, but he didn't say anything as we stood there, using up all the water. I wanted to stay there forever because somehow, I felt safer than I'd felt since Thalia died. And she'd been gone for what felt like an eternity.

"I don't think you told us the full story of what happened in Canada," Dom guessed, breaking the noise of the running water. "You didn't just lose your friends, did you?" My non-answer was confirmation enough. His hand rubbed along mine and I felt happy and sad at his touch. "I was supposed to be mated." That made me lift my head slightly, with my cheek still pressed to the middle of his back. "I fell in love with a Born vampire girl when I was young, and I proposed as soon as we were out of high school. Our parents said we were young, but we didn't care. Her name was Jade." I felt the sad smile in his voice. "When..." His voice broke, and he stroked against my hands to steady himself. "When the sharks came, a pack of them overwhelmed us and they killed her." He breathed in a ragged breath and sniffed a few times. Slowly, I lifted one of my hands and entwined my fingers with his, shooting a tingling lightning bolt up my arm.

"Thalia..." I faltered slightly because I'd never spoken her name out loud since her death. "She joined our group after two years had passed since the mass turning. We got along so well, it felt completely natural when we became a couple. I would've taken my vows then and there and become mated to her for eternity." My tears mixed with the water on Dom's back. "Thalia died protecting humans from the sharks, she took her last breath right in my arms." My arms tightened around him and I felt my ribs contract with the pain of losing her all over again.

Dom let my hand go and turned to face me. His warm hand came up to stroke my cheek as he studied me with his blue and brown gaze, and he leaned down slowly enough where I could've stopped him if I wanted to, only I didn't want to stop him, and when he hovered just above my lips, I captured his with my own and we kissed under the shower of warm water with a passion that rivaled that of my parents.

20

THERE'S ALWAYS TIME TO FLIRT

KITTY

*A*fter we'd dried off and gotten dressed again, we left the showers to see Shadow licking himself by the empty pool.

The life-altering kiss we'd shared was making me feel awkward, so I avoided looking at Dom as much as possible while I climbed into the empty pool and set my tent up inside it. Dom had his own sleeping bag, but he didn't bring a tent with him. Tough luck, sir. My tent only sleeps one. Me. You and your pity kisses that made my toes curl can sleep outside. I got inside my tent and zipped it shut to keep him and Shadow out. Dom rustled with his stuff, setting up his sleeping bag and getting something to eat from his backpack, dried fruit by the smell of it.

"Thank you," he said after we'd been silent for at least thirty minutes. "I know telling me about Thalia wasn't easy.

You're not the type to share with just anyone. You're exactly like Arthur, in that sense." *Humph.* Awfully pretentious of him to presume things about me. Even if he *was* right. "I hope I'm worthy of that trust." With the tent fabric in the way, I couldn't see his face, but I could tell by his shadow he was looking in my direction. "Maybe we could kiss again and make it better?"

"No kisses, or anything else," I said quickly, moving away from the tent door. "I'm not in the habit of kissing strangers. You don't even know me."

He paused, and I felt my pulse thumping along my throat. "I'd like to." When I didn't answer, mostly because there was a lump in my throat, he laid down on his sleeping bag and I saw Shadow curl up next to him. "I'll be here waiting, and when you're ready for more, let me know."

As if.

It took forever to fall asleep, maybe because of all the pent-up energy I'd gotten from thinking about Dom's smooth, beautiful lips, or maybe because I wasn't sure if I hated the idea of him unzipping the tent door and kissing me again, even though I was still terrified about it. Gods, I felt like a teenager again, stressing over boys and crap. I didn't have time for this. I had to find my brother, and we had to return to Salvation to make sure my family wasn't killed in the rebellion. There was no room for anything else.

I didn't realize I'd dozed off until a loud *bang* echoed off the walls of the pool, snapping me awake. Jumping up, I grabbed Artemis and almost ripped my tent apart unzipping the door flap. Dom was sitting on his sleeping bag, opening a can of food with a can opener, and he looked up at the twin barrels of my gun.

"Don't shoot," he joked, and tossed me one of his cans of food. "I dropped mine, sorry if I woke you up." He handed me the can opener when he was finished, his can wafting with the scent of baked beans, and my can turned out to be the same thing. I started eating, avoiding Dom's face, and we both scooped out a handful for Shadow at the same time, smiling timidly when we saw the other doing it. "I've fed from the bleeders, so let's get going as soon as we're done."

I nodded and took a mouthful of beans, chewing and letting the savory flavor of bacon and maple syrup fill me. I definitely wanted to get used to eating real food again. "Were they all drugged out?" I saw him nod with a frown out of the corner of my eyes. "Too bad we can't get them to donate more to bring with us. We don't know where the next bleeder town will be. I can make it on shark blood, but you can't."

That's when Dom smiled at me and I raised my eyebrows, looking over at him finally. "I might've negotiated further once they'd sampled the goods." He shrugged unapologetically and patted a fabric ice chest next to him he must've had in his bag. "Brought it with me just in case. It has a battery pack I can recharge to keep the blood cool."

"You sneaky git," I appraised with a grin, and he shrugged a second time, matching my smile.

I wanted to kiss him again.

No! We weren't doing that. We had to find Jason.

We finished our canned beans and left the pool with Shadow at our heels. The humans were all asleep in the bar, so we left them where they lay and drove out of town. With both of our stomachs full, we wouldn't need to drink again for days if it came to it. I was used to being thirsty, and I assumed Dom was as well.

Driving down the unending roads, I could feel Dom's breath against my neck, and it made every nerve ending on my body feel like an open flame. To say I was frustrated by the time we made camp was an understatement. Dom brought out a hand crank and plugged it into his cooler to charge the battery. He cranked away at the handle while I set up my tent.

"Don't suppose you'll share that tent with me tonight?" he asked me, looking away to not seem obvious.

"If I do, that's all I'll be sharing." He nodded distantly and cranked more, the sound much louder than I liked. We didn't want a shark invasion on our hands. Every so often he checked the battery percentage and continued cranking. Shadow sat next to him, his ears twitching from the noise as he tried to fall asleep.

Despite the racket Dom was producing, the night was still and quiet, and I enjoyed the lull in our journey as I chewed on some jerky and stared at the night sky. With the city lights gone, I could see the smoky clouds of the Milky Way, all purples, blues, and pinks. I'd seen it every night for twenty years, but I'd never actually sat and stared to appreciate the beauty of it all. It wasn't in my nature to stop and admire the roses, but maybe, after all this was over, I could finally stop moving long enough to do so.

Dom checked the battery one more time and stopped cranking, satisfied with his work. He set the crank back inside his backpack before moving past me to crawl inside the tent I was sitting in front of, barely brushing my leg and causing a shot of heat to go over me.

"Ahhh, comfy," he said once he'd laid out his sleeping bag and gotten comfortable. With a turn of my head, I saw him fully zipped up into his sleeping bag like a vampire burrito. "See? I'll keep my hands to myself."

I wasn't worried about him keeping *his* hands to himself. I was worried about my growing need to put *my* hands on him.

Shadow joined Dom in the tent, and with one last look at the sky I did as well, bringing our bags in and zipping the front up. I wasn't fully joking about the tent being only for one because we were squeezed together inside with hardly any space left. I put my head where Dom's feet were and got comfortable with my little pillow, even though Shadow was perched right at the apex of my thighs to keep warm. I reached a hand down and pet at his head, and he started purring.

"Now would be a great time to make some kitty jokes," Dom joked in a whisper, and I knocked my hand against his leg in punishment. "I'll behave, I promise. But I give great foot massages, just in case you're interested." I pulled my feet away from him and he laughed behind his hand. "I'm sorry, I can't help it, Kitty. You're so easy to tease."

Humphing, I rolled over to face away from Dom, upsetting Shadow. "I don't have time to flirt. I have to find my brother."

"There's always time to flirt," Dom retorted, but he didn't speak again until I fell asleep.

21

SHARK ATTACK

KITTY

"*J*t's definitely broken," Dom pronounced, his head on the ground beneath my motorcycle.

I kicked at the dirt, bringing up a cloud of dirt. "*Damn it,*" I swore, kicking more in frustration and letting out several swear words for good measure.

"Let's stay calm, kitty cat," Dom suggested unhelpfully.

"*What did I say about calling me that?*" I hissed at him.

"That you'd empty a round into my... *cajones?*" I groaned for a good ten seconds and started pacing the dirt road. "We can still walk. We're almost to the Texas border, it won't take long to get to the farmhouse. Maybe a few weeks."

"*Weeks?*" I shrieked, turning sharply towards him and bringing up another cloud of dirt. "I don't have *weeks*. My family could be hurt, or arrested, or dead. Or all three."

Getting up, he dusted his jeans off and pat his hands

together to get the dirt off them. "Your mother sent you on this mission because of that. She knew they were in danger, and if they didn't make it, at least you'd have your brother." He picked up his bag and started down the road without me.

I stomped my foot in anger. "Where are you going?"

"Here, kitty, kitty, kitty," he beckoned to me with his middle finger up.

Gods *damn him*.

I picked up my bag and left the broken motor cycle on the road. She'd served me well for many years. I'd miss her. Still, I had Artemis, who would come in handy if Dom called me kitty cat again.

"I spy with my little eyes," Dom joked once I'd caught up with him.

"A dead man?" I offered, smiling sweetly.

He pursed his lips and reminded me of the way Knight looked when he was mock offended. "You're not going to kill me, kitty cat."

Grrrrrrrr.

"Pray tell, future corpse," I ground out, kicking at some plants on the cracked pavement.

"Because if you're ever in a bind, I'm your only food supply." He pointed a finger gun at me with a thousand-dollar smile.

Taking a deep, measured breath, I gave him the courtesy of not shooting him.

"I feel the need to remind you how short tempered the women in my family are."

"A fact Arthur mentioned often," Dom said with a chuckle. "He *loves* your mom's temper."

With a groan, I clamped my hands over my ears. "*Lalala*, I don't need to hear that."

Shadow ran ahead of us and jumped from one large pile of pavement to the next in a black blur, only stopping to munch on the green grass every so often, because that was the food of champions. Or he needed to throw up. Either way.

We walked side by side for hours, and while Dom tried to keep up the conversation, he eventually pulled up his skull mask to keep his mouth clean from the dirt in the air. While I was ecstatic for the silence, it was also penetrative, and I didn't want to fall inside the pit of my thoughts.

Oddly, I wasn't thinking of Thalia at all. Somehow talking about her out loud had let me finally gain perspective on losing her. No, I was thinking of Jason, and my vision of him sickly and alone. Was that what awaited us?

Maybe he was dead.

What would I do if he was? What if I went back to Salvation and they were all dead too? I'd be alone again. And this time, there'd be no quest for my missing family to hold me together.

Immersed in my thoughts, I tilted my head to look at Dom beside me with his face half covered by a skull mask and his blonde hair so covered in dirt, it was almost a different shade. He might stay with me. The question was, did I want him to?

Dom blinked several times and reached a hand up to wipe

at his eyes. Without goggles like mine, dirt was dotting his vision and he stumbled on a large pile of roots covering the road. I reached out for his hand and caught him before he could fall.

"Thanks," he said, still trying to clean his eyes out with his dirty hands.

I came up close to him, so close our breath was mingling, mostly so I could block the dusty wind from his face. "We should try to find the closest supermarket. They'll have goggles so you can cover your eyes." He nodded, and still holding his hand, I led him down the road, keeping in front to try and block the dirt as much as possible as Shadow followed behind us.

Our little caravan made it to a supermarket just before dusk, and we barricaded the doors before exploring the vast building. Shelves of packaged food, racks of clothes, and all the things a good supermarket needs awaited us. Most was aged with time, but since the building was still intact and the doors had been closed, it kept everything clean from the ever-blowing dust bowl.

"Meet you at the furniture," Dom announced as he sprinted off toward the home improvement area.

I didn't necessarily need anything since I tried to keep my bag as light as possible, so I walked slowly amongst the various items, running my hand along the sleeves of blouses and grabbing some tanks tops when I spotted them. Realizing the opportunity, I filled my backpack with a few clothing items I needed to replace. Once I was done, I spotted the books across the aisle from the women's clothing.

In the popular theme of my life at that moment, I wondered just how long it had been since I'd read a book. Looking back, it had been before the sharks came. I'd never loved reading as much as mom did, but I didn't hate it. Abandoning the clothes, I crossed the aisle over to the shelves of paperbacks, and when I ran my hands along their slick covers, I felt sadness at the stories that would never be read. The adventures that would never happen.

One stood out to me, a colorful volume with a grumpy fairy on the cover. I took it and slipped it into my jacket. Maybe I'd find time to read it. Shadow jumped up onto the shelves and started rubbing against the magazines. Bending at the waist, I gave him a scratch under the chin and went to find Dom. My nose led me past the greeting cards and craft supplies to the auto area where Dom was trying on some ATV goggles. Not as stylish as my steampunk ones, but they would work.

We walked to the furniture and unboxed two mattresses to lay out on the linoleum tiles. I opened the fairy book and started reading it as Dom stretched out on his mattress, staring up at the industrial ceiling like it was the night sky.

"Night, Kitty," he whispered, and within minutes I heard his breathing and heartbeat slow, a very soft snore coming from his mouth. Normally I'd have stayed up to keep watch, but I felt safe enough to finish reading my book and fell asleep with it on my chest.

———

BANG!

A loud crash startled me awake and I jumped up with Artemis in my hand. Another crash came, prompting me to kick at Dom's leg to wake him up. Letting out a groan, he rolled over and opened his mouth to complain at his mistreatment, his accent so thick I could barely understand him, when more bangs rang through the air. I pushed my senses out to see where it was coming from and...

"*Sharks*," I muttered, and my pulse started thumping against my throat. There was a horde of them outside the supermarket, the crashing noise was their rotting bodies running into the glass sliding doors to try and get inside.

Dom must've pushed his senses out too because he scrambled up and let out a string of swear words as he gathered up his things. I shoved my book inside my bag and started reaching for Shadow to zip him into my jacket when the sharks broke through the glass doors and stampeded into the store faster than a herd of antelopes. Shadow ran in fear of the commotion and I chased after him, towards the horde of sharks.

"Move your tail, kitty cat!" Dom shouted at me just as I'd managed to grab Shadow. His cat claws scratched at my impenetrable skin, but that was a mere distraction from the sharks coming right at us. Dom pulled at my elbow and we ran down the medicine area, back to the gardening section. The growls and stomping feet of the sharks were closing in on us, only spurring our effort to get the glass doors open, and just as we'd gotten them apart, the sharks descended and we fell underneath their sheer mass of bodies.

Teeth tore into me and Shadow ran from my arms when I couldn't hold him any longer. The sharks had me like a football player at a buffet. Blood spilled, turning the air bitter with the smell, and I pushed through the pain enough to start attacking my assailants back. For every bite they gave, I gave two more. I tore, I pulled, I threw, until the sharks were off me and I could stand up. Dom was under his own pile of the monsters and without even thinking, I flung out my claws and dove in like a tornado.

Even with many of the sharks falling under my claws, the horde was so massive, I knew this was a losing battle. I reached a bloodied Dom under the sharks and pulled him along with me by one hand, beating off more sharks with the other. We slipped through the crack in the doors and somehow got out of the metal garden corral before the sharks could come after us. I chanced one look back at them and saw their arms reaching through the space between the sliding doors, desperate to get us under their teeth again. They were too stupid to move aside and squeeze out of the doors to come after us.

Dom was able to stand once we were safe for the moment, and I took his hand as we raced off away from the store.

"This is a fine time for our cycle to be broken," I complained through gritted teeth, pulling Dom along through the parking lot. Somehow, Shadow had also made it out, and he galloped along with us. I picked him up because he couldn't keep up when we went full speed.

My senses still pushed out, I felt the crack of the glass doors inside my chest like someone had just stepped on me with a large boot. The sharks pressed against the glass so hard that it shattered like the first set of doors.

"Incoming!" Dom shouted, and the flood of sharks once again started chasing us, free from the barrier. Even with our head start, it wasn't long before they were gaining on us. We were running so fast, I was starting to feel winded, as impossible as that sounds. Somehow Dom found enough breath to say, "If we don't make it, I enjoyed kissing you."

"Shut up and *run faster*," I hissed at him.

Dom tugged my hand and he pointed to a brick building with a rusty fire escape that looked like it was about to fall apart. He steered us towards it, and I handed Shadow to him so he could go first. The stairs groaned under his feet, but he ran up them so fast they didn't break under his weight. He punched out a window on the third floor and threw Shadow inside before turning back to me.

I'd waited too long, trying to make sure they were safe, and I stared up at Dom's duel-toned eyes before the sharks descended on me like bees on a flower. I went under like before, but this time I couldn't fight my way back out. They bit me, they tore at me, and my blood flowed like a crimson river.

I passed out.

22

OH, BROTHER

KITTY

I didn't expect to wake up. Somehow, I found myself opening my eyes to see an abandoned apartment around me. Dom stood at the broken window, Shadow sat on the kitchen table, and I was on a purple couch.

Everything hurt.

The more I came to, the more I smelled blood in the air. My blood. I looked down at my hands and they were covered in a thick blanket of red. More importantly, one of my pinkies was hanging off by a sliver of skin. I groaned and Dom turned from the window, quickly crossing over to the couch. He pressed against my shoulders to get me to lie back down.

"Stay put, you're injured," he cautioned me, and kept pressing until I lay flat on the sofa.

My throat didn't seem to work properly, bringing a slice of pain when I tried to speak, so I only got one word out.

"Hurt."

Dom's eyes were etched with concern, and I knew I was much worse than wounded. Before I could register it in my brain, my hunger rose from all my injuries, and I felt a frenzy creep its way up to me. My fangs dropped, my eyes glowed, and I heaved out each agonizing breath. Without hesitation, Dom helped me sit up and pulled me into his embrace on the coffee table.

"Take what you need," he whispered into my ear, sending a responding shiver up my spine from being so close to him.

I sank my fangs into his neck as easily as slicing butter, and his blood tasted like pure sunlight. I'd never tasted blood like his before, not even Thalia's. I wanted it every day, filling me with its golden beauty so I'd never have to drink from sharks again. Dom's hands curled up on my jacket and I drank deeply of his essence, every mouthful pure ecstasy. Once I felt better, I retracted my fangs and licked his already healing skin clean. My pinkie restored itself after I pushed it back to my hand.

"You taste amazing," I breathed against Dom's neck, the words slipping out before I could stop myself from saying something like that. "It's been so long since I had vampire blood, I think I forgot what it tasted like."

"Of course I taste amazing. I'm awesome." He held me closer to him, and with my hunger gone, I enjoyed being near him. The intimacy of feeding was a pleasant excuse to be in his arms, if only for a moment.

"Have the sharks gone?" Normally they'd stay around, but

with the fresh corpses we'd left at the supermarket, the sharks would gravitate there once we were gone. My fingertips absently ran up the bumps of Dom's spine before I realized what I was doing. It felt natural though, being there with him.

"Took several hours, but they've all left. Your blood must've been like a vampire twinkie. I've never seen them stay that long before with fresh kills nearby." I felt his fingertips on my spine now, sending another shiver up it, and my cheeks reddened from the response.

"We should go then, they'll come back if we stay too long." Despite my words, I stayed motionless in Dom's lap.

"Yeah," he echoed, but he also didn't move. My heartbeat betrayed how much I liked being this close to him, but his was beating just as fast, drumming out a rapid duet that neither of us could hide.

Shadow broke the spell with a jump onto the coffee table, meowing loudly at us. We broke apart and busied ourselves with packing up again and giving Shadow water before we left the building. I cleaned myself off with some wipes, enough where my bloody smell was diminished. Muted, but still there, it attracted several sharks on our way out of town. We dealt with them as they came and continued on our way.

⊶

USING KNIGHT'S DIRECTIONS, it took us almost a week to find the right area in the giant state of Texas. The biggest indicator was the smell of dog piss, a common way of marking

Lycan territory. Once we'd found it, Dom and I both winced and held our masks to our noses.

"His?" Dom asked under his mask. I shrugged. Piss is piss. You can't tell whose it is by smell. Or maybe you could if you were a Lycan, but I wasn't. It was still a good sign, however, sparking us to walk faster down the roads.

My stomach fluttered in anticipation and my heart seemed to leap out of my chest when I caught a second scent, a real non-piss one.

Jason.

A cry escaped my lips and I took off running closer to the source of the smell. Dom ran beside me, perfectly matching my speed and powers. We were made to run together. We could take down anything by each other's side. Shadow meowed inside Dom's jacket, protesting our above human speed, but Dom's hand over the kitty's head protected him from whiplash.

Jason's smell got stronger and I saw in the distance the old farm house I'd seen in my vision, Knight's childhood home. Stopping at the top of a hill, my lungs seemed void of air, and it wasn't because I'd just ran for miles. Even with my brother's scent in my nose, I was still afraid of what I'd find in the farm house, but I'd spent too much time worrying about what might be. I jumped off the hill and ran down a field of wildflowers, the farm house getting closer and closer with each step.

I slowed down outside the porch, Dom coming to a stop beside me with a whoosh of air. He let Shadow out of his jacket and the cat ran off in protest of our treatment of him. It barely registered with me, because I could hear a heartbeat behind the front door.

Jason definitely wasn't dead.

A dog barked loudly from inside the house, and the door opened sharply to show Jason standing with a shotgun barrel aimed at us. Dom put his hands up in surrender, but I didn't bother. Jason wouldn't shoot me.

Far from the gangly teenager I'd known, he was a grown man now, with muscles for days and his impossibly curly long hair, turned slightly brown from being in the sun. The most important bit was that he appeared healthy and strong, not at all like I'd seen him in my vision.

"Kitty?" he questioned when he saw me, looking very unsure if I was really there or if he'd dreamed me up. How long had he been alone? I didn't smell anyone else in the area, and that was telling.

I took off running again, straight up the stairs and into my brother's arms. He was taller than me now, towering over me like a skyscraper. I clung to him, sobbing against his white shirt, and he ran his fingers through my long curls, holding me so tightly I thought my bones would break.

"My baby brother," I cried against him.

"Watch who you're calling baby, Kitty," he joked, his voice much lower than before. I looked up at his deep, brown eyes and smiled with relief. At least they were still the same. He reached a dark hand up and wiped at the tears on my cheek.

"Mom and dad here?" He looked up for them, petting my hair again.

"That's a bit of a long story, mate," Dom said from behind me.

Jason leaned down and kissed me on the top of my head. "I'll make some tea."

23

THE UGLY SIDE OF LIFE

KITTY

The inside of the farm house looked nothing like my vision. Jason had made it a real home, with furniture and a working stove he put some firewood into before lighting it with a stone flint. He placed a kettle full of well water on top of the cast iron burner and reached inside a cabinet for some homemade tea packets.

"The apocalypse is going strong, and people still have tea," Dom commented, placing his chin on the top of my head. I shoved him away before Jason could see.

"An Aussie, eh?" Jason said with a grin. "Haven't seen an Aussie vampire in a long time."

"Can't very well live where you might burn to a crisp," Dom joked, and Jason laughed under his breath as he fixed a snack for us. He motioned for us to sit at the small round kitchen table and brought over some fresh fruit while the tea boiled.

While eating cantaloupe slices and peaches straight from the trees outside, we told Jason all that had happened in the past twenty years. He didn't comment on any of it, just nodded to show he was paying attention, and he hopped up when the water was hot, pouring us glasses once the leaves had steeped long enough.

"So you're going back to rescue everyone?" he asked, sitting down with his cup after pouring ours.

I nodded and took a sip of my tea. It was a mango mint mix, and it took a few seconds for my tongue to adjust, but it was actually pretty good. "As soon as we can. You should pack up, and we'll leave before dark."

"No."

I choked on my next sip of tea and set my cup down to clear my air pipe. "Excuse me?"

Jason was staring out the kitchen window, his mind miles away. "I'm not leaving here. You can go without me."

"*Que mierda*," I swore under my breath. "I just found you after twenty years and you're telling me to get lost?"

A darkness spread over his face that I'd never seen before. "That's exactly my *goddamn* point, Kitty. I've been on my own for the better part of twenty years, and where were you? Gallivanting off with your girlfriend and looking for mom? Screw you. You could've found me easily and you didn't even try." He stood up sharply and knocked his tea over, stomping over to a window on the other side of the kitchen, the spot I'd seen him sitting in during my vision.

"That's a bit harsh," Dom admonished while watching Jason walk away.

"I don't need a stranger commenting on my family matters," Jason snapped behind him.

What had happened to him to make him like this?

I stood up hastily and my legs bumped the table. "Fine. I'll leave." Jason stiffened from his spot at the window, but he didn't turn. "Just so you know, mom is pregnant with Knight's baby. Your full-blooded sister. Our sister." A tear rolled down my cheek as I stared at his back. "She's having another vaewolf. If we don't rescue her, our sister will be raised in bondage. She'll never be free."

"She?" Jason asked quietly.

I shrugged where he couldn't see. "I guessed." Dom stood and squeezed my shoulder with his hand. "If we make it out of the city, I'm coming back for you. And if I never return..." My voice faltered and I swallowed to get it back. "I hope you're happy here."

I left out the front door, ran all the way through the field of flowers, and I didn't stop for anything.

I'D FINALLY FOUND my brother and he didn't want to come with me. The thought consumed me while I ran and ran across the Texas countryside. I didn't stop to see if Dom was behind me. What did anything matter now? My family might be dead, my brother refused to stay with me, and my father was still gone.

With tireless energy, I ran for days, using up all the blood Dom had given me until my stomach growled in protesting hunger. Shut up, stomach. I'm not stopping until my feet refuse to keep moving. Maybe then everything would make sense again.

My marathon ended when I entered a small deserted town and I tripped on a piece of broken pavement, face planting onto the ground. Then I just lay there, motionless, and I cried salty tears of regret, remorse, and reminders of my failings. The sun set and rose, but I stayed there on the dirt where I belonged. I closed my eyes and finally let myself drift off to sleep after days with no rest.

My nap was interrupted from a boot to my stomach, and I woke up with a growl to a circle of bleeders grabbing me by my arms and putting vampire cuffs on my wrists. Bleeders had invented them during the early days of the turning, when humans were still afraid of us. Well, I say still. They would never really stop being afraid of the monsters they shared their world with.

Damn bleeders had my *gun*, I realized with another growl.

They dragged me down the street and up to a building with open doors, an old meat packing plant by the looks of it.

"Kitty!" I heard someone shouting down the road, and the

bleeders turned me none too gently to see Dom running down the pavement, Shadow nowhere to be seen.

"Looks like we're double lucky, boys," one of the bleeders said with glee. He pointed his rifle at Dom when the vampire was close enough, and Dom raised his arms in surrender. The other bleeders took him and slapped on another set of vampire cuffs. With us restrained, they took us inside to a metal storage room and slung our cuffs onto strong hooks that ran from the ceiling, our arms suspended above our heads.

"It's a shame there wasn't a Lycan with you two," the head bleeder said with an evil grin. "Our last supplier... expired." I fought against my bonds at the thought of a Lycan suffering with these bleeders. The ceiling hook stayed put, and I knew it had been made to withstand a vampire or Lycan's strength.

"I'll rip all of your heads off, you shriveled up—"

The bleeder cut me off with a backhand across my face. "Shut your mouth or I'll muzzle you," he warned, and I shot him the deadliest glare I could conjure as he turned to pick up something from one of the metal tables. A bucket and a tube. My many years of travel had taught me things I never wanted to know, and I knew exactly what the bleeder was about to do. I struggled so hard I felt the skin on my wrists slice open against the cuffs and blood trickled down my arms. The bleeder noticed and smiled again. "Maybe you'll behave yourself now."

"No!" I shouted with more struggling against my bonds, but he ignored me and brought the bucket and tube over to

Dom. He took a special knife from his pocket and used it to slice across Dom's leg. Dom cried out in pain and the scent of his blood filled the air. I was so distracted, it didn't even make me feel thirsty. The bleeder stuck the tube into the cut he'd made, preventing Dom's body from healing itself, and Dom's blood started flowing into the bucket. *"I'll murder you,"* I ground out to the bleeder. "You'll die a thousand deaths before I'm finished with you."

Unfazed, the bleeder checked his handiwork and straightened, throwing me a grin. "We'll see."

Distracted or not, I eventually could hardly think with the smell of Dom's blood in my nose and my stomach rumbling from hunger.

"I'll be fine, kitty cat," Dom joked with a pale smile, and he turned his dual-toned eyes up, nodding to comfort me, like I was the one having the life drained out of me. Every second was an eternity, but finally the bleeder was satisfied with the amount of blood in the bucket and he pulled the tube out of Dom's leg before leaving us alone in the metal room. Dom managed a weak smile. "Saving some of us for later, ehh?" His skin went even paler and his head dipped to his chest.

I swung my leg at him, but I could barely reach his side. "Dom, stay awake. You can't fall asleep." If he went into a frenzy, the bleeders would shoot him. I'd never get to see his smile again or stare up into his blue and brown eyes. And I realized that would've made my despair that much worse.

With no way to mark the passage of time, I didn't know how long we were in that room. The bleeders came in several times to take our blood, refusing every request to let us down. Hunger was starting to overtake both of us, and I didn't know how much longer I could survive without blood. Thankfully, the bleeders eventually brought in two bags of blood and Dom tore into his as they held it up to his face, but I turned my nose up at mine.

"I don't drink human blood," I informed them tartly.

The bleeder grabbed at my hair, making me wince in pain. "Then you can starve." He left us and I slumped my head against my chest. My arms were on fire from the abuse. I would've done anything to be unchained.

"We'll get away, I promise," Dom said weakly. He was worse off than me, having given extra blood because he was more docile than me. I still found the strength to fight and kick at our captors when they came at me with their blood bucket.

I appreciated Dom's heroism, but I found it ridiculous. We were too weak to escape. My arms hurt so much, I couldn't even contemplate trying to move them.

"Guess we won't save everyone after all," I joked wearily, sagging against my bonds.

Dom stilled and tilted his head to the side like he'd heard something I didn't. "Never say never, kitty cat."

"Wha..." My blood reserves were so depleted, I didn't have enough to use on my senses. Before I could hear what he was hearing, he started panting and I turned my head sharply at him.

He was going into a frenzy.

"Dom, no! Fight it. You can't slip away from me." Salty tears flowed from my eyes, despair filling me to the brim. "Dom..." I swallowed the lump in my throat and said exactly what was in my heart, because if we didn't make it, I'd never forgive myself for not telling him. "I should've let you kiss me again. I want to kiss you so badly, even right now with you looking like death warmed over." Dom's eyes fluttered open and he looked at me hazily. "If we're not making it out of this, I want you to know that. I want you in my life, even if we've only just met. Will you stay with me?"

His mouth curved into a smile and he shuffled his shoes on the floor to turn his body towards me. "Well now I definitely have to survive. I'm not passing up a chance to kiss Kitty Bathory again."

I smiled at him, and I felt a small sliver of happiness, here where our story was coming to an end.

Fate had other plans, and the door to our room burst open as Jason came in with two smoking pistols in his hands like a warrior from heaven. Dom growled, pulling at his bonds with Jason's blood calling to him. Jason gently picked me up by the waist and unhooked my arms from the meat hook, the sharp pain from the blood rushing back into my limbs making me cry out. He set my feet onto the ground.

"I'm sorry I let you leave, Kitty," he confessed brokenly, holding me close. "I'm so sorry."

"Don't let it happen again, stupid face," I sauced weakly. Jason turned to Dom and I stopped him with my burning fingers. "He's close to a frenzy. We can't let him loose with you in here."

"Kitty," Dom ground out, panting with the effort, his eyes just barely turning red. He was right on the edge. "Won't... hurt him... let me... go..." Jason reached up to unhook Dom and I stepped in front of him just in case Dom attacked. He fell to the ground and ran out of the room without stopping. Jason picked me up again, slinging my arm over his shoulder, and we left the metal room behind.

We found Dom face first in a pile of bleeders Jason had shot on his way in to rescue us. Dom finished drinking all of them dry and he stood, wiping his very bloody mouth with his jacket sleeve. He panted and nodded to me like it was a normal day.

"Your boyfriend is gross," Jason commented, and I flicked him with my finger to shut him up. After un-cuffing ourselves, we left the building to see three motorcycles outside by a hitching post like a cluster of mechanical horses.

"Nice, you got us motorcycles," I observed happily, eyeing the biggest one lustily.

"Not exactly," Jason said, and set me down on the pavement, holding me up with his arm. "I didn't tell you what happened to me."

"*Que?*"

As an answer, three masked figures appeared from a building across the street. Women, by the shape of their bodies. One had long, straight brown hair, and her scent made me pause. She was a vaewolf like Jason, part vampire and part

Lycan. The second had blonde hair in a long braid, and her scent was known to me: Marie, my mom's vampire secretary from before. The third drew my attention so much I almost did a double take. She had long, black curls and pale, white skin. On their approach, each woman took off their goggles, the last revealing a pair of familiar purple eyes.

"Grandma?"

24

I'M SO SHINY

KITTY

My journey to find my family had led me to the only person I hadn't looked for, and she was sitting across me at our makeshift camp.

Anastasia Bathory, the crazy vampire who had slaughtered hundreds of vampires and Lycans in her insane spree of vengeance and spent hundreds of years in a comatose state after giving up my infant mother to keep her safe. Did I mention she was crazy?

Marie, who last I knew was more interested in designer heels instead of polishing a gun, was doing just that against a nearby tree. She finished her work and my grandmother stood to join her. Anastasia pulled Marie in by her hips, giving her a triumphant kiss, not unlike my mom making out with Arthur.

In shock at the sight of my grandmother kissing *Marie* of

all people, I looked at Jason to see if he shared my surprise, but he was smiling, *smiling*, at them.

Oh my god Marie was mated to my grandmother.

With that tidbit stored away, I cleared my throat and they stopped face sucking long enough to come back to our circle.

"Jason has told me everything about Lisbeth and the human city," Anastasia said once she'd sat down again.

"Including the part about my mom having two lovers now?" I wondered how she'd feel about that.

Anastasia shrugged and fiddled with one of her long curls in thought. "I've had several lovers at once, many times."

I grimaced and wished I hadn't said anything. "I'm going to pretend that's not gross to hear." She shrugged again and Marie took some of her black hair to put in little braids. "How did you get here so fast, by the way? Where were you?"

Anastasia raised her eyebrows at Jason who looked away in avoidance. "Jason did not tell you."

"No, Jason did not." I turned to him accusingly and waited for him to look up at me. "He told me to piss off before I could find out what he's been up to for the past twenty years."

"I..." Jason sighed and scratched at his neck. "I said I was sorry. I haven't had it easy, and sometimes it's hard to interact with people."

"How about I start. You were with Balthazar, my bio dad," I offered, flipping my palm up in a signal for him to continue.

"We went to an island west of California. He was there with me for several years, helping me grow food and keeping me company until..." My heart stopped and I reached for his hand, to comfort myself more than him because I had a sinking feeling where this was going. "The Bicus came, they arrested him for reproducing after the ban was in place. They had Toni in custody too. Took him away to the Bicus plane. I never saw him again."

And that's exactly what I thought he'd say, which was *great*. My dad had been thrown in prison for creating me. My anxiety rising, I squeezed at Jason's fingers and he kissed my fingertips to get me to let go before I broke his hand.

"After that, I had to fix the motorboat we'd used to get there and come back to the mainland. It broke at some point, so I had to swim the rest of the way. I floated up to a beach, as exhausted as I'd ever been, and I wandered around for a long time, trying to find someone who would take me in. Dad used to tell me about the farm house in Texas, so many times I felt as if I could find it in my sleep. When it was finally in sight, I was bloody, dirty, and tired enough to fall asleep for a year. That's how I stayed until Anastasia found me."

"First thing I did was hose him off," she said with a grin. "I didn't know he was my grandson at first, just that he needed my help. He'd been alone for many years." Just like me. "As soon as he was old enough to be on his own, I left to continue my search for Alistair."

The mere mention of the man was enough to raise my hackles. He was the one who had ruined the world.

"Alistair? That's where you've been all these years?"

She nodded and sipped at her canteen. "He's a slippery one, but I finally found him with the help of Marie here."

"I trust you made him pay," Dom inquired beside me.

Anastasia's mouth curled and I couldn't tell if she was gleeful or remorseful. Both. Hauntingly, both. "He won't hurt anyone again."

We all relaxed with a collective breath, from something I didn't realize I'd been worrying about.

"He had Yukina as a prisoner and we brought her with us," Anastasia continued, gesturing to the brown-haired girl who had been silent this entire time. From the first glance, I'd known she was a vaewolf like Jason. He'd been staring at her off and on as we left the town and made camp in a patch of trees, like she was a priceless artifact he'd been searching for his entire life. He was a love-sick puppy, and his scent was very telling about the nature of his feelings for her, I can say that much.

My stomach took that moment to growl loud enough to wake up a bear during hibernation season. Jason laughed at me, I punched his arm, and Anastasia stood up.

"Come here, you can drink from me."

Oh god. My mom had told me stories of Anastasia's heightened powers. She didn't even need to blood binge to be the most powerful vampire ever. What would drinking her blood be like?

Gulp.

I got up and crossed over to her as she removed her jacket and pushed her black t-shirt to the side, revealing her pale, smooth neck. Hesitating only a little, I leaned in and took a small sniff of her scent before I sank my fangs into her neck.

OH MY GOD.

If Dom's blood was pure sunshine, Anastasia's was like taking a bite of the actual sun. It was like a thousand shots of espresso, with a hundred energy drinks, and Night Shadow without the hallucinations. I pulled off after getting a stomach full and gasped with a burp-cough.

"Holy shit," I exclaimed, my eyes widening to saucers. "I feel high. Can I get high from your blood? Am I talking too loud? Oh my god I'm so shiny right now."

She was trying not to laugh at me, patting my back with a smile. "You'll be fine for awhile now. I can't say how long, I've never fed a vipyre before."

My stomach flipped over, and I held a hand to my mouth to keep my dinner from coming back up. "Check please." The feeling passed before I'd sat back down between Jason and Dom. I looked at Dom and started brazenly stroking his chin. "You're so cute. I like your face."

"Maybe my blood is too much for her," Anastasia said in thought. Mmmm, no way. I wanted her blood more often.

"We should get to bed," Marie pronounced just as I was about to lean in and kiss Dom on his cute little lips. "We have to get to Salvation as soon as we can. We have no idea what's been going on there since Kitty and Dom left them."

I hoped it was all good and shiny things.

25

PLANS FOILED

DREYA

*A*s my three parents plotted our next move amidst some passionate make-out sessions on the couch, I was having my own make-out session on the clock tower balcony. Darius' hazel eyes somehow shone brighter than his pink aura, and I drowned in them with every kiss to his soft lips from my perch on top of his lap. Stopping for air, I pressed our foreheads together and ran my fingers through his brown curls.

"I could kiss you forever," he breathed, moving his lips down my cheeks and to my neck where he kissed every inch of my skin.

I wish I could've seen my own aura. I wondered if it was as pink as Darius' was. Or if it was pink at all. That hardly mattered, and I giggled at his tickling kisses on my ear, pulling my head away from him. Whatever I could say about him, he was a good kisser.

"I want to tell you something," I told him with a grin. My parents had been against this, but I trusted that Darius was in love with me and would do whatever I said, even if I didn't have mother's psychic abilities to make him do whatever I wanted. I checked his face first, saw the full pink of his aura, and kissed him on the lips again to seal his mood. "My father is here."

His smile remained, and I felt hopeful for a moment. "Knight? Is he in the stair landing? Do you have to go home?" He turned to look through the hole in the clock, but I pulled his face back to me.

"No, not Knight. Arthur. Arthur is here."

When his smile fell, my stomach plummeted ten stories. "Arthur is a fugitive, Dreya. He was banned from Salvation for drug possession." The pink was slowly turning to green, and I almost saw red on the edges. Trying not to panic, I kissed at Darius' hands, anything to see the loving pink again.

"It was a long time ago, he's not on the stuff anymore, I promise. He just wants to be with me again. Can't your dad forgive him?" I kept my face as innocent as possible, and Darius eventually shifted back to a very light pink, but I knew he wasn't in the mood for kisses anymore.

"I'll talk to him," Darius said, running a hand through my hair.

Sighing with relief, I leaned back on my knees. "Sorry I ruined the mood," I apologized with a shy grin.

He smiled at me and gave me a gentle kiss on the lips. "It's fine. I have something for you, actually." Reaching into his pocket, he brought out a small box and handed it to me. Inside was a silver necklace with a gold ring on it. "It was my mom's," he explained, slipping the band onto the tip of his finger. "Dreya, I know we're young, but I know how I feel about you. I want us to be together forever."

And at that moment, I knew I was bathed in the brightest yellow that ever touched the sky.

"I WISH you'd gone with Kitty," father said for only the fifth time in the past twenty minutes. With my fingers gripping the chained ring underneath my dress, I suppressed the desire to roll my eyes as we continued walking down the darkened street. In the past week or so we'd gotten to know each other a bit, but he still treated me like a child. It was something I could forgive because he had never raised a kid before, but it was still *god awful* annoying and tested even *my* patience.

Resisting the urge to tell him to shove it, we arrived at our destination and Arthur knocked on the door three times before it opened to reveal Olivier dressed in a simple black dress, bathed in angry red light as she always was. Olivier's subdued wardrobe was enough to raise my eyebrows, but we walked in before she shut and locked the door behind us. Renard sat at their kitchen table and she gestured for us to sit across from him while she made us something to drink.

"Dreya, always lovely to see you," Renard greeted with a smile and a nod to me, the surrounding light above him a mix of yellow and blue. He stood and pulled Arthur into a hug that my father did *not* enjoy before letting him go. "Never thought we'd see you again, you old barracuda!" We sat down before Arthur could behead Renard, and Olivier served us some orange juice in big tumblers.

"I never thought I'd be plotting a coup again with my ex-boyfriend, Arthur," Olivier said into her glass.

"*Again?*" Renard snorted, coughing on his drink. His mate simply shrugged and went on sipping her juice. Arthur had briefed her on the situation a few days before, tonight was simply discussing our next move.

"I'm betting Lisbeth is unwilling to leave any of us behind?" Olivier guessed, drumming her fingers on the wooden table. Arthur nodded and she rolled her eyes. "Bleeding heart, that one. She might be terrifying in her fits of rage, but she's soft as a kitten otherwise. No offense, Dreya." I shrugged because she wasn't wrong, even if I didn't agree with her thoughts on leaving everyone else behind. I saw the merit in it, since our, or rather my life was on the line right now. If our small group left, we could get reinforcements and take Salvation over as soon as we were ready. Mother was unmoving on the matter, and she insisted she'd rather stay a prisoner than make everyone else one in her stead.

"I still have to stay in the shadows, and it limits my scope," Arthur grumped. "I need you two to start questioning the guards, see who's on our side and who's not. Hendrix has several of us loyal to him. I suspect he's even created a few dhampirs, though I've never seen them."

Olivier squeezed at her glass so hard it cracked on the side and Renard took it from her before she could break it. "He's made *dhampirs?*" She said the word like it was an unholy swear word, so bad even the pope wouldn't utter it. It was followed by a tirade in French and the few words I knew brought a quick blush to my cheeks. "None of us would give him one *willingly*, Arthur. We're not even allowed to make our own children. If a vampire gets pregnant, we're not allowed extra blood and the baby dies." Renard gently took her brown hand and squeezed it, making her colors shift slightly pink.

They couldn't have their own children since Renard was a turned vampire. I'd often wondered how they coped without the option, but not everyone wanted babies. I kind of did, I suppose. I was far too young for it, but I could picture it. Little blonde-haired babies with crystal blue eyes. Or maybe they'd inherit the black curls and purple eyes that skipped me over.

Unbidden, the image of a baby with Thomas's green eyes came to me, and I grabbed my tumbler of juice to take big gulps in an attempt to wash the image away.

"The problem isn't just who's under Hendrix's control. He has human soldiers too, and they have guns that can hurt us," Renard pointed out before taking another sip of juice. He ran a hand across his bald head and down to his red barbell mustache that he stroked in thought. "Bullets aside, we're stronger, even if they out number us."

Arthur's orange juice lay untouched, but he stared at it like it was a crystal ball that might tell him the outcome of this battle. "We should strike at night, when they're most vulnerable. They'll be tired, weakened, and they can't see in the dark like we can."

A crash came from outside making us all jump. Arthur knocked over his glass and Olivier dropped hers on the floor where it shattered.

"Get Dreya home, *now*," Olivier hissed in warning, and Renard led us to the back door while she picked up the pieces of glass. We scurried out the back door and Renard closed it behind us, leaving us in the dark alleyway. Were there rats here? I couldn't see any in the corners of the alley, but it smelled rank, like something had died in here. Arthur's colors rippled with gray and green, and I felt his concern when he took my hand and led me down the dark alley. We reached the end, Arthur checking both sides before we walked into the empty street.

"We should talk to Darius, I'm sure he knows who's loyal to Hendrix or not," I whispered in a very low tone so any humans couldn't overhear us. Arthur was leading us away from the clock tower, probably just being overly cautious, but it made my stomach feel like it had a thousand knots, and my spine tingled with hot dread like something bad was going to happen.

Maybe I should've gone with Kitty. I wasn't cut out for espionage, and every move I made was putting my life in danger.

"I'm not trusting that boy with anything," Arthur said firmly, as he had been for the past week. I pouted at his aura, watching it turn red.

"He might surprise you, you know."

"Doubtful," Arthur scoffed, and I really wanted to kick his shin bones to make his aura even more red. He continued leading us down dark paths and between buildings.

"If you'd listen to me, I don't think we even need to use force," I mentioned, as I had several times. "Darius could help us. He might even be on our side if we tell him all that his father has done."

"*SSSH,*" Arthur shushed sharply, as I'd gotten too loud. "We're going to see Thomas, and I don't want to hear more about your boyfriend."

I was about to kick at his shin bones after all when a flood light switched on, turning the dark night into a brightness I had to shield my eyes from.

"Arthur Lancaster, you are under arrest for violating Salvation city limits," a loud voice came over the announcement intercom. The speaker squeaked several times, making my ears hurt.

We were surrounded by soldiers, and something about them made me pause. Humans? No. Not humans. My senses were overwhelmed from the lights, but my nose was fine. Their smell was off, and I remembered what that meant.

"*Dhampirs,*" Arthur ground out beside me. Hendrix had an army of dhampirs. Stronger than humans, and loyal to the governor. We were *so* screwed.

"Hands up," the intercom shouted. We complied, and two dhampirs came up to cuff Arthur. It wouldn't have been enough to hold him down under normal circumstances, but he complied for my sake.

A figure came from the dhampir ranks and I struggled to focus enough in the light to see who it was.

"My son told me you were here."

Hendrix.

I'd trusted Darius, and he betrayed me. All that hard work winning him over, making him love me, it was all *wasted*.

"Darius assumed that his innocent little Dreya had no idea what her father was doing, but I did. Visiting Olivier, gathering support. Tut tut, Arthur. Didn't anyone tell you to not plan an uprising when your family is on the line?" Hendrix turned to me and he looked me over with none of the kindness I'd seen from him before. "My son was a fool to trust you. You and your traitorous family. I should've killed your mother when I had the chance." He sniffed the air like he could smell something beyond the steel, dirt, and fear. "Take Arthur to prison with the others. And you." He crossed the distance between us and roughly took my arm. "You're coming with me."

26

PRISON BREAK

KITTY

*W*ith only three motorcycles, we had to pick partners. Marie, of course, wanted to ride with her snuggle puss. Jason was still following Yukina around like a lovesick puppy, despite his denials of the fact, so they were together as well. Dom and I were on the third, and I was happy to be back on a bike and speeding down the highway instead of walking. Having Dom's arms around me was nice too.

I was still waiting on that kiss I'd told him I wanted. I was unwilling to do so with my brother and grandmother in the mix, because unless we were miles away, they'd hear us. Jason's sarcastic high fives to our parents every time we caught them making out came to mind, and I wasn't about to be embarrassed by him. Then again, if he ever tried to tease me about

Dom, I could always tell Yukina he had the hots for her already, after just meeting her.

Had Jason even kissed a girl before??

The thought ran through my head as we sped down the road towards Salvation. Maybe it was good they'd found Yukina. Jason deserved another creature like him, one that wasn't our sibling. My heart hurt that he'd been as alone as I had over the many years since the sharks came.

One thing I knew, neither of us would ever be alone again, and we'd make it back to Salvation to save our family. We had to.

The journey was painstakingly slow. I felt like a snail trying to crawl around the world before dinner. Though we had speed on our side, it still took several days to get there as our cycles weren't as good as my old one and didn't hold a charge for longer than four hours.

I. Was. Going. Insane.

"Calm down, kitty cat," Dom soothed unhelpfully beside me. We'd set up camp for another slow, grinding night, and the others were away gathering supplies at the nearby town.

"We're moving like a turtle, Dom. We need to be there *now*." I paced the leaf covered ground, my boots rustling them with every step. Dom came up to me and held my arms in a vice to keep me in place. With him so close, I felt the tension inside me coil up like a viper, and wet tears of frustration trickled down my cheeks. "What if we're too late?"

He leaned in and kissed my forehead. "Then we'll raze that city to the ground, kitty cat. I won't let them hurt your family without punishment." He smiled down at me and my heart pounded in my chest.

"When are they coming back?" I asked absently, focused on his pink lips.

Dom took in a breath when he caught the change in my scent, and his pupils dilated, making my pulse race under his gaze. "No idea."

"Cool."

I stood up on tiptoes and pulled him in for a kiss that made every nerve in my body come alive. Everything was right with him by my side. Our kiss deepened, prompting me to work us backward to my tent where we zipped up the door and things progressed to a toe tingling level very quickly.

THE NEXT MORNING, Jason was waiting for me with a smirk and a high five, and I resisted the urge to punch him right in the nose. Dom's scent was different, as was mine, the result of our night together. There was no trying to hide it. No one else commented because they had decorum, unlike my brother.

We left our camp behind and drove the last length of four hours the bikes would take us. I knew we were close to Salvation, so close I was itching like there were ants in my pants. Dom and I guided everyone to Simon's camp to leave our bikes.

Clara and Lucas were there waiting for us, and they

grabbed Anastasia in a hug that lasted a good five minutes. Clara planted kisses over her twin sister's cheeks a dozen times, cooing soothing words in their native language. I doubted they had ever been apart for so long, not in all their five hundred years. The two took Marie in their embrace like a sister as well and hugged her for a long time while whispering how much they'd hurt her if she betrayed Anastasia.

Once our greetings were out of the way, we geared up and the Lycans came with us on the long road to Salvation. Dom on my right, Jason on my left, I led the group with Artemis on my hip. It was a moment that needed really awesome theme music, as Knight would've said if he were there.

The city's fence came into view on the horizon and I picked up my pace, trying not to run but eager to get there faster. When we came within scent range, I saw half a dozen soldiers standing guard at the gate. Dhampirs.

"Were they there before?" Jason asked as we took them in. I grimly shook my head. Governor Hendrix had created dhampirs. That rutting son of a hamster. Who had given birth to them? Which of our kind and his did he force? He was going to *pay*.

"Let's go," Anastasia ordered, stepping ahead of me with purpose. She was just as angry now, and she was terrifying enough when she *wasn't* pissed off.

As soon as we approached the gate, the dhampirs we on alert with their guns out. They had masks over their faces that covered their necks from us. I didn't need a neck to drain them dry. I'd never drunk from a dhampir before. Would it be enough for me? I'd love to find out.

"Surrender all weapons," they ordered us as more dhampirs came from inside the city. We begrudgingly handed over our guns and knives to them, and then they slapped cuffs on us. Cuffs again? I didn't like the way this trend was going.

Cuffed and disarmed, the dhampirs led us inside the gate and it closed behind us with a mechanical whirr. We got pat down, just in case, and once they were satisfied, it was time for the walk of shame. The dhampirs led us through the heart of the city, past all the bleeders and their hateful glares. Several threw things at us and shouted that we were monsters.

Damn straight, I'm a monster. And I'm coming for all of you.

It felt like the dhampirs had purposefully walked us by every bleeder in the city because the walk went on forever. Finally, we reached a guarded door on the north side of the compound. The dhampirs standing outside it opened the doors and we were shoved inside a dark, dank room lit only by torches. *Torches.* What was this, 1830? *Peasants.*

By the torch light, we walked down a hallway and it opened out into a room that smelled like metal, mildew, urine, and blood. My eyes adjusted and I held in a gasp. They'd led us to a prison, and the only prisoners were vampires and Lycans. All of our brothers were either locked in cells or chained to the walls.

"Move," one of the dhampirs ordered before he kicked at my legs, making me stumble. Dom caught me and we walked further into the room. Right in the center, chained spread eagle was Olivier, foaming at the mouth like a rabid dog at the sight of the dhampirs.

"*Je vais assassiner chacun de vous et pisser sur vos os*[1]," she spat venomously at them. She tended to revert back to French when she was beyond furious. Like right then.

"Should've muzzled that one," a dhampir complained at her loud musings that were still going on as we walked closer to her.

"Kitty!" she shouted when she saw us. She struggled at her bonds, but they held her down so tightly she could barely lift her head. "Jason!"

"Jason?" another voice came from one of the cells, and Knight came to the front of it, his face obscured by the thick bars.

"Dad!" Jason exclaimed at the sight of him. Arthur was in the same cell and came forward to see us. They were chained to the wall of their cell by a cuff on their necks.

"Stop talking," the dhampir soldier next to me shouted, and he kicked at me again, sending me whirling to the cell wall where Knight and Arthur were. I righted myself with my hands on the bars and both of my dads were baring their teeth at the guards for roughhousing me.

"Where's mom?" I asked before the dhampirs took me away.

"Hendrix," Arthur answered, glaring at the dhampir that roughly grabbed my arm. "You hurt her, and I'll rip your arms off." The dhampir laughed, *laughed*, and took me to the wall next to the cell to lock my neck in a metal cuff before taking the cuffs off my wrists. They locked Dom beside me and the rest of us along the same wall. Jason got to the end of his chain once the dhampirs had left us alone, just barely able to put his fingertips on the cell wall that held our dads. Knight reached out and they clasped wrists outside the bars.

"You good, son?" Knight asked, his voice trembling ever so slightly at the sight of Jason.

My brother nodded and wiped at his nose with a laugh. "Yep." He looked at Arthur and held out his other hand for the vampire to take, which he surprisingly did almost immediately after it was offered. "Hear you're my second dad. Welcome to the fam."

"I don't respond to the word '*fam*,'" Arthur grumbled.

Knight wiggled his finger against Arthur's shoulder. "You're stuck with us now, sunshine. No take-backsies."

"Leave it to you to find humor in this place," Olivier hissed. Renard was chained next to her and he was massaging her arms to combat the loss of bloodflow.

"At least I'm not yelling in French how I'm going to murder them and piss on their bones," Knight countered, sticking his tongue out at her.

I stood next to Jason who was still holding Knight's arm like a lifeline. "Where's Dreya?"

"Hendrix," was Arthur's repeated response. I gripped the bars so hard I hoped they snapped in half.

"Ana," Knight muttered when he finally noticed his

mother-in-law chained beside Jason. She stood and came as close as she could to us.

"Kitty, drink my blood again. You and I are escaping with Clara." She pulled Marie to her for a kiss, and they whispered loving things as a farewell.

"What about them?" I demanded, gesturing to my family. "I'm not leaving them behind."

She rolled her eyes at me. "We're not leaving them. We'll get the keys from the guards and they'll help everyone else escape." Oh. "Are all the vampires and Lycans in here?" she asked Knight. He nodded, and she nodded back in confirmation. "You two will get everyone out of the city limits safely."

"Ordering everyone around like usual, ehh mom?" Knight joked, and instantly regretted it when she glared at him. "Sorry, ma'am."

Without missing a beat, she exposed her neck for me and I latched on like it was a line of sugar to snort. *Happy shiny sugar.* I was full within moments and tried to pull away, but she put her hand to my head. "More. You need to be stronger." I obliged and drank until she let me stop, then she turned to Clara and drank from her twin for her Super Saiyan power up while I started spinning like a Ferris wheel, *wheee*! Once she was done, she kissed Clara's forehead and broke through her sister's cuff like it was paper. "That's better. I was about to kill them for hurting you." She broke hers as well and turned to me expectantly.

Me? Break a vampire cuff? As if. I put my hands on the cuff, my fingers sliding between the metal and my neck, and gave it a yank. It broke with little effort and I stared at my hands in awe. I was *Super Kitty*! I flexed and drew Dom in for a kiss.

Arthur made a noise of complaint when he saw us. "That's not why I sent you with her. *We're having words later, you pissant.*"

"Sssh, it's so cute!" Knight squeed. "Psst, Dom. You hurt her and I hurt you." He smiled and held a thumbs up to the man in my arms.

"We're wasting time," Anastasia admonished, and Knight deflated with a pout. "Let's go, Kitty."

I left them all behind as the three of us walked back down the hallway to the heavy metal door. Anastasia knocked on it like that was normal in this situation, waiting patiently for it to open. The dhampir guards were taken aback by the sight of us, but Anastasia raised her hands and they instantly stood at attention.

"Keys," she ordered them. One produced some keys that would unlock all the cuffs in the prison. "You will go inside this building and free everyone before coming back outside to your post. No one escaped, you saw nothing. Got it?" He nodded and disappeared behind us to the dark hallway. "And you," she addressed the second dhampir. "Everyone is still a prisoner, you didn't see anyone escape at all. Right?"

"Yes, ma'am!" he shouted dutifully, and turned back to his post at the door like nothing had happened.

"Let's go," she said to me, and we were off down the street.

THE REIGN OF TERROR ENDS

DREYA

"*Y*our food is going to get cold, Dreya," Governor Hendrix chided. We sat at his dinner table, mother and myself, both out of place amongst the dhampir guards. Darius wasn't there, he'd been confined to his room so he wouldn't help me escape, and don't mistake me, he would've if I'd asked. Despite his betrayal, I had him wrapped around my finger, even if Governor Hendrix thought differently.

I managed a polite smile, plastering on the practiced patience I'd had for my entire relationship with this miserable man's son. "It looks delicious, Governor." Beside me, mother ate her portion of noodles and tomato sauce without comment. She hadn't spoken a word since everyone had been locked away, and I feared she would enter the comatose state her mother had been in so many years ago. If she did, I'd be on my own, and only my ties to Darius would keep me safe. If that.

The Governor turned his slimy gaze to her, showing a purple color that made me feel sick. "You've been silent lately, Lisbeth. I've known you long enough to know you always have something to say." She remained silent, eating the last remnants of her food and placing her fork on the plate to signify she was finished. His mouth twitched in irritation, but he still smiled at her sickeningly. "I've decided to approve the union of our children," he announced, looking back at me. *Yes.* All my hard work would be worth it. "It will forge a new bond between our species, and we will work toward fixing all the hurt feelings your rebellion caused. Who knows? Maybe after a few years I'll release your mates if you behave yourself."

Lisbeth's blank face wasn't giving anything away, but her aura shone the brightest red I'd ever seen. It was brighter than any red Olivier had ever shown, brighter than Arthur's red the day he was taken away when I was a child. It was so red, so encompassing, it made *me* angry just looking at it. Very far underneath the red was a gloomy blue that tore at my heart. I didn't know anyone could feel equal portions of anger and sadness at once, but she was proving me wrong.

Mother's hand moved to her belly where Hendrix couldn't see. My little sister would be born into this life. I had no doubt Hendrix would take her away as soon as she was born, if she would even be allowed to survive long enough to *be* born, and either of those things would be the last straw I could take.

"When will I get to see Darius?" I asked the Governor brightly, putting on my best face. "I can't wait to start planning our wedding."

He smirked at me and took a sip of his water. "You're not going to see him at all. Your marriage is only for the public. I won't have you corrupting him behind my back. Don't think for a second I buy your little act. You're Lisbeth's daughter, after all."

My hopes fell from their tower and smashed down to the ground like a delicate vase. All my hard work. Everything I'd sacrificed. It had all been for nothing. I'd never see Thomas's smile again. I'd never hold him in my arms and tell him I never liked Darius, how I'd only dated him to ensure my family's safety. And I'd never get to kiss Thomas, like I'd wanted to for so many years.

"Don't talk to my daughter like that," Lisbeth clipped in a dangerously quiet voice, her spine suddenly straightened and her head tilted in a way that meant she was listening to something in the hallway. I was too low on blood to hear anything, but the anticipation inside me rose.

Hendrix raised his eyebrows and smiled at her. "She speaks! I was beginning to—"

"Shut *up*," Lisbeth ordered, slamming her fist on the table, not enough to break it, but our glasses shook so hard some water spilled out. Hendrix waved the guards away from us when they came forward in response to her movements. Her face went blank, but I could see the red overtaking her entire body. She was only rage, only anger. "Decades ago, a vampire named James held me captive as you have. He tortured me every day mercilessly, and the worst part was I could not refuse him. He had me under his control, in a way that was worse than your attempts to control me. I swore... I *swore*, that if anyone else ever tried to control me like he did, that I would fight back, that I would break free. And you came, threatening my daughter, ripping my mate from my hands, and holding my husband's life over my head like he was a bug you wanted to squish for your personal enjoyment."

A single tear rolled down her cheek, the only betrayal of the emotions I could see swirling all around her.

"James *never* hurt me the way you have."

I covered my mouth to hold in the tears I felt coming over me. She was so still, like a statue. A dangerous statue with the red around her growing deeper and darker with every word she spoke. Even Hendrix was looking uncomfortable at the sight of her.

"Alistair ruined the world for vampires, Lycans, and humans, and he wasn't as cruel as you," Lisbeth continued evenly, her fingers curling around her slightly swollen belly. "My mother slaughtered hundreds of my people, and she was still more merciful than you. You alienated me from my husband for years, you made me afraid to even open a window. I haven't felt the sunlight on my face in thirteen years. You killed..." Her voice faltered slightly as despair filled blue overcame her, but she continued. "You killed my brother and sister. Before the drones came, vampires destroyed my home brick by brick, and you came and destroyed me stone by stone. I will not allow you to continue your destruction with my children. Dreya will not marry Darius."

Hendrix scoffed and sat back in his chair. "You have no room to make demands."

"I'm very certain I told you to *shut up*," she retaliated, and he cowered slightly, enough where I felt satisfaction at his fear. She stood and the dhampirs responded with a step forward until they were all frozen in place. "Now, mother."

Before I could ask what was happening, Kitty burst in with two women. One held her hands out and the dhampirs moved out of the room under her command. From their descriptions and the telling purple eyes, I knew the women were my grandmother and her twin sister.

"Under Hendrix's personal orders, the vampires and Lycans are to be freed. He's transferring control of the town to someone who isn't a complete moron," Anastasia compulsed, and the dhampirs continued down the hall out of sight under her orders.

"You can't just—" Hendrix complained before mother cut him off with her hand around his throat. She leaned over him, pulled the pistol out from his belt, and dragged him over to the middle of the room where we stood around him, all pulling out our guns. Anastasia handed me her second pistol and I clicked the safety off as I'd been taught.

Anastasia, Clara, Lisbeth, Kitty, and Dreya Bathory. We all

held a pistol to the head of the man who had tortured my mother for so many years.

"Your reign of terror is over," Lisbeth proclaimed. "This city will never again hold my people prisoner."

Collectively, we let off our shots like a firing squad.

28

FOR AS LONG AS I CAN

LISBETH

Lisbeth

Six years later.

*

It was a warm, spring day in Texas at the farm house. I fluttered around the kitchen, making sure everything was just perfect for my daughter's special day. Celebrating birthdays was something I'd gotten used to while living amongst humans, and while I still never enjoyed mine, I couldn't imagine my years without a birthday party for my children. A new year was something to celebrate. It meant another year with family, another year to learn and grow and love.

"Is the cake done?" Arthur asked as he came into the kitchen and tenderly kissed me on my lips, sparking the flame that I would never take for granted again. I deepened our kiss and I forgot the cake in the moment, immersed in his love. Since he returned to me, we hadn't gone a day away from each other. I could barely even stand him leaving to take a shower. If I could've permanently attached him to me, I would've done so eagerly. No amount of time would erase my need for him, nor his for me.

He smiled down at me, something he reserved only for our private moments, and I cherished it like a precious gem. He pulled me closer and kissed me again, deeply, slowly, forgetting why he'd come inside except to kiss me. "Cake," he said finally, coming up for air.

"It's almost done," I breathed against his lips with a smile. I turned, still wrapped in his arms, and ran my spatula over the pink icing to finish the smooth edges before I sprinkled some chopped nuts on top. Arthur kissed at my neck, right where his bite was. "You're going to distract me again," I chastised him, not that I was complaining.

"I have to get all my kisses in while Knight is away," he reasoned with another kiss on my neck. "He'll just steal you, and I need all of you for every moment of every day."

I giggled. "You know you love him in your own way. I've seen the way you look at him. It's almost hotter than kissing you."

"*I do not look at him.* Shut up." I turned in his arms, smacked him, and pulled him in for another kiss. "Don't tell him, he might take it wrong. He's not into men."

I laughed again and wiggled out of his arms to pick the

cake up. "Let's shelve that conversation for when we're not at a family party." He grumbled, his hands clutching the back of my skirt, following me past the wooden dining table and out the front door with our black cat, Shadow, at our heels.

Outside was a birthday party for my fourth child, Guenevieve, Gwen for short. She was turning five today, and we were celebrating it in style.

After leaving Salvation behind, we'd settled into the farm house of Knight's youth. There was a human town nearby with various settlements of vampires and Lycans from the city that had come with us. We all looked after each other, in the way Salvation should've been. Over time more humans had come, and while not all of them were ecstatic about having vampire and Lycan neighbors, we kept the sharks away, and that kept us on their good sides, mostly.

At our farm house, Gwen was playing chase with Jason and Yukina in the front garden. The two had been inseparable since they'd first met, and while we didn't exactly do weddings anymore, I knew they would've said their vows without any hesitation.

"Come and get me, Gwen!" Yukina shouted playfully, jumping onto Jason's back as they ran around the grass.

Gwen's little brown legs tried to keep up with them and her black curls bobbed around, having escaped from the braid I'd put them in. She was a carbon copy of Knight and had inherited his brown eyes, meaning she only had to pout at me once and I did whatever she wanted. She squealed when she saw me putting the cake onto our lawn table and ran up to me, grabbing my legs.

"Mommy!" she shouted happily. "Is daddy coming back soon?"

I bent down and kissed the top of her brown head. "He'll be here, I promise." She let me go and held her hands out to Arthur for him to pick her up as I started putting some tiny homemade candles into the cake.

"Dada!" she shouted when Arthur had hoisted her up into his arms. She pulled at his cheeks and he almost smiled at her. Almost.

An engine came in the distance and I perked up at the sound, the cake forgotten. Arthur followed me down the driveway as Jason and Yukina came up beside us to watch the truck arrive.

This day wasn't just Gwen's birthday. No. Today was even better. I brought my hand up to my mouth to stifle my tears and the truck came close enough for me to smell everyone inside. Arthur shifted Gwen to his right arm and he put his left around my shoulders.

"They're here," I sniffled, tilting my head to rest against my mate's. They were finally home. The truck came up to us and stopped with a swerve to the left. Behind the wheel, Knight waved to us, but the back of the truck unloaded before he could get out.

A bombardment of my family came at me and I was swept up in a wave of hugs from everyone who'd been gone for the past five years. Dreya, Thomas, Kitty, Dom, Anastasia, Clara,

Lucas, Olivier, Renard, and behind them was the man who'd been gone for much longer than them, the man they'd gone searching for while we held up the fort.

Balthazar stood with his cane in hand, smiling up at me with his smooth as silk grin, as he always had before we were parted.

"Traffic was hectic in Copenhagen. Sorry I'm late."

"You *bastard*," I shouted at him, taking off in a run and grabbing him in a tight hug. The relief I felt with his arms around me was almost surprising, but I was still angry with him, and I pulled away to shout my frustration. "Getting yourself thrown in prison, making my family have to go after you, you jerk wad, I am so pissed at you, and I know my grandmother is up in heaven calling you every name she can think of because you're such a *jerk*!" I caught my breath after my tirade, and I held him even closer, kissing him on the cheek over and over. "I'm so happy you're home." Toni the succubus was waiting in the truck bed, watching us. She waved at me with a small smile, a complete change from her usual demeanor. Maybe they'd been in prison for much longer than it had been for us since time moved differently in the Bicus realm. I released him from my hug and wiped my nose, turning to hug Knight when he came up beside me.

"I smell cake," he noted with a sniff, looking around for it. I loved him so much. At least he hadn't been gone for five years, I wouldn't have been able to bear it.

"Stupid Bicus realm and its *stupid* time warping. We were there for like twenty minutes and came out five years later,"

Kitty grumped, Dom's hands in her jacket pockets from behind. He kissed at her head and Shadow the cat came to rub against Kitty's legs. "Then we came out in a weird place, and it took us days to light the signal beacon Arthur set up nearby so Knight could come and get us."

"I haven't eaten in a *week*," Dreya complained in Thomas's arms, finally displaying her real self again.

"There's *cake*," Knight emphasized in response, pointing in the direction of the smell. Everyone left us to go grab slices of it and some of the fruit I'd left on the table. Knight stayed behind to give me a tender, slow kiss on my lips, and I felt warm and happy all over. He swished our noses together cutely and kissed the tip of mine before folding me into his arms. "All mine," he proclaimed with a smile.

"Close, but no," Arthur corrected beside us. I heard him set Gwen down so she could run after Kitty.

"Ssssh, daddy's talking," Knight smarted. I knew Arthur would be rolling his eyes at him, and I giggled against Knight's chest at the mental image. I turned just enough to see him, in fact, rolling his eyes, and I reached out for his hand, which he took and accompanied it with one of his secret special smiles. Knight looked up and the smile disappeared, but only just. "Did you think when you came to arrest this rabble rouser that you'd end up falling in love with her?"

Arthur didn't even pause. "Absolutely not."

"What?" I bleated in complaint.

He inclined his head toward me, almost smiling again. "But I'm glad I did."

"Close enough," Knight proclaimed, and he took my other hand to lead both of us to the lawn table where he claimed the last three slices of cake for us.

I watched my children chasing each other on the lawn, the adults laughing at a story being told, and my mates standing on either side of me. We'd been broken, abused, and had loved ones taken from us forever, but in that moment, we had each other, and that was better than any vision of the future, because this was the future I wanted to live.

For as long as I could live it.

NOTES

6. THE PRISONER

1. *Cabrón:* Bastard

26. PRISON BREAK

1. *Je vais assassiner chacun de vous et pisser sur vos os:* I will murder each of you and piss on your bones.

Glossary

*B*icus: A collective term for the sibling creatures known as Incubus and Succubus.

Bonding ceremony: A vampire wedding involving a vow between the couple, exchanging of each other's blood, and mixing their blood together through a cut on their wrists.

Born vampires: The product of an Incubus and human female union. They can turn humans, create drones, and give birth to new vampires. Born vampires must drink fresh human blood every day. Drinking bagged human blood cannot sustain them and will cause them to slowly starve.

Companion: A term for the humans that serve vampires. They sign a ten year contract and are chosen by a vampire to live in their rooms, and be willingly bitten once a day to feed the vampire. Once their contract is up they can either renew it, or they can leave with a promised sum of money upon contract termination.

Council: A group comprised of the heads of each vampire Order. They oversee all vampires, pass judgement for infractions, and direct the vampire Hunters.

Dhampir: The product of a vampire and human union. None were known to exist as the two species typically do not mix romantically.

Frenzy: A state vampires reach when they are so starved of blood their body can no longer cope. They become wild, their eyes glow red, and they will attack until their hunger is sated.

Hunters: A group comprised solely of Born vampires whose sole purpose is to hunt down any vampire that has broken the law, and either bring them to justice or execute them.

Incubus: A creature of seduction, built for the sole purpose of coupling with female humans to create new Born vampires. If an Incubus falls in love, they develop a distinctive scent.

Lycans: The product of a Primal werewolf and human female union. They can shift into a wolf whenever they like.

Primal werewolves: Originally human men who have been scratched by a succubus, turning them to a werewolf when the full moon rises.

The Bicus plane: A mystical realm only accessible to those with the blood of the Bicus. Time moves differently inside the plane, moving slower or faster than Earth depending on the moment.

The Order Acilino: Location in Spain, name translates to "Eagle."

The Order Bête: Location in Canada, name translates to "Beast."

The Order Dedliwan: Location in Australia, name translates to "Deadly."

The Order Engel: Location in Greenland, name translates to "Angel."

The Order Gennadi: Location in Russia, name translates to "Noble."

The Order Janiccat: Location in Malaysia, name translates to "Born."

The Order Khalid: Location in Algeria, name translates to "Immortal."

The Order Oleander: Location in the United States, name translates to "Poisonous."

The Order Qiángdù: Location in China, name translates to "Strength."

The Order Raposa: Location in Brazil, name translates to "Fox."

The Order Safed: Location in India, name translates to "Undamaged."

The Order Sangre: Location in Mexico, name translates to "Blood."

The turned vampires: Vampires that used to be humans and have been. Note: the word "turned" in reference to this type of vampire is never capitalized, hence referring to them as "the turned" to avoid this. They cannot turn humans, or give birth. The turned must drink human blood every day. Unlike the Born vampires, the turned vampires can survive on bagged blood.

Vaewolf: The product of a Primal werewolf or Lycan and a vampire union. They can shift into a wolf whenever they like, they have vampire fangs, and they require blood to heal if they are seriously injured. They do not require daily blood like vampires do.

Vipyre: The product of an Incubus and vampire female union. An incredibly rare creature, only one has ever been known to exist, but it is most likely due to lost knowledge as these creatures have been written about in Incubi lore.

Bathory Family

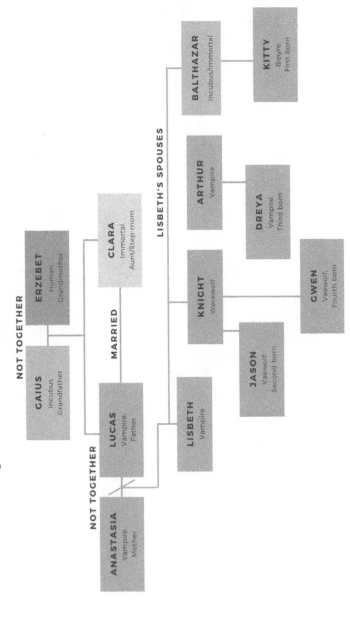

NOT TOGETHER

GAIUS
Incubus,
Grandfather

ERZEBET
Human,
Grandmother

CLARA
Immortal,
Aunt/Step-mom

MARRIED

NOT TOGETHER

LUCAS
Vampire,
Father

ANASTASIA
Vampire,
Mother

LISBETH
Vampire

LISBETH'S SPOUSES

BALTHAZAR
Incubus/Immortal

ARTHUR
Vampire

KNIGHT
Werewolf

JASON
Vaewolf,
Second born

KITTY
Bixpyre,
First born

DREYA
Vampire,
Third born

GWEN
Vaewolf,
Fourth born

Castle of the Order Oleander

Road to town

Front gate

Underground
Garage ramp

Social
Area

Cliff-sized
Chessboard

Picnic
Tables

Back gate

Christening
River

ABOUT THE AUTHOR

Photo by Elizabeth Dunlap

Elizabeth Dunlap is the author of several fantasy books, including the Born Vampire series. She's never wanted to be anything else in her life, except maybe a vampire. She lives in Texas with her boyfriend, their daughter, and a very sleepy chihuahua named Deyna.

You can find her online at
www.elizabethdunlap.com

CPSIA information can be obtained
at www.ICGtesting.com
Printed in the USA
LVHW041540231120
672481LV00003B/611